INVADE THE HEIGHTS

INVADE THE HEIGHTS

THE HEINOUS CRIMES OF SARA SLICK™ BOOK 4

ST BRANTON   CM RAYMOND   LE BARBANT

DISRUPTIVE IMAGINATION

LMBPN Publishing
PMB 196, 2540 South Maryland Pkwy
Las Vegas, NV 89109

First US edition, July, 2020
ebook ISBN: 978-1-64971-045-1
Print ISBN: 978-1-64971-046-8

THE INVADE THE HEIGHTS TEAM

Thanks to our Beta Readers
Larry Omans, Kelly O'Donnell, Allen Collins

Thanks to our JIT Readers

Paul Westman
Diane L. Smith
Kelly O'Donnell
Deb Mader
Angel LaVey

Editor

SkyHunter Editing Team

Rand looked out over the faces staring back at her. Fingers cracked, and necks rolled. Anticipation filled the air like the sizzling of electricity. War was coming, and they would be the galvanic heroes. Under her direction they would lead, they would win, and they would conquer. They itched for blood. The single unifying vision of glory permeated the room and filled the Philosophers, making them sweat in their hunger for direction.

Most of them, anyway.

They waited for her to tell them what was to come, what she expected of them. Among the other Philosophers, Bentham watched her carefully.

Rand knew there could be no hesitation. The plan had already begun. There was no stopping it now. Bentham secretly worried the same thing.

"The Harbingers have started an all-out assault. We're getting reports of *Pax* violations on every continent. The Guild is handling it, but on behalf of Guild leadership, I'm giving the official order for my top Agents to focus on only one thing. Bringing in Sara Slick."

A slight murmur filled the room.

"Is that a wise choice?" Bentham questioned. "Sara Slick is only one person. Wouldn't it be better to focus on keeping the spread of violence and damage to a minimum? If it's as bad out there as you say, we'll need all hands on deck to maintain the *Pax*."

Rand turned to Bentham and stared into her eyes for a moment before responding.

"Every major incident of the last year has had Sara Slick in the middle of it. There is no reason to believe she's not involved in this newest set of atrocities. This is our chance to stop her." She drew herself up and looked at each of the people in front of her purposefully. "By stopping her, we can stop the Harbingers."

"I'm sorry, ma'am, but that doesn't make sense. Sara Slick doesn't control the Harbingers. Our intel suggests they hate her as much as we do. I don't understand how putting all our efforts into—"

"It never ceases to amaze me what you don't understand, Bentham," Rand snapped, cutting her off. "Your inability to grasp the purpose behind this mission and its subtleties is beside the point. You will do what needs to be done."

Rand's expression suddenly went cold, and a cruel smile edged onto her lips. She continued, "Unless, of course, your commitment to the Guild is wavering. You don't want us to question your dedication to your duty, do you, Bentham? After all, you've let Slick escape your grasp many times."

Bentham squared her shoulders.

"You don't need to question anything. My duty has always been to the Guild and peace, as has my loyalty. You can trust my commitment. I will do what needs to be done."

"I'm glad to hear that." Rand looked out over the rest of the group. "Listen to me and listen to me carefully. We are at war. Anyone who disobeys will be considered a traitor and treated accordingly." She looked at Bentham again. "Is that fully understood?"

Her team responded with an enthusiastic yes, which was how Rand liked it. She didn't accept doubts from those beneath her, not when the world was at stake.

"Stay vigilant. Summon whatever strength, courage, and resolve you can. Sara Slick's days are coming to an end."

CHAPTER ONE

"Come at me, you fucking octopus!"

Not the most elegant of battle cries, I'll admit. But in my defense, my mind was occupied by the many arms of the blue, bulbous mass bearing down on me. I can't always yell something poetic when I punch shit like this.

It didn't seem happy with my response.

While it might not have been a malevolent octopus summoned from The Deep with an intent to murder me, it was a damn fine fighting machine from The Far. It swung one of its long, muscular appendages in my direction and crunched into my ribs, sending me tumbling back into the wall of the subway car.

"What the hell is that?" came a voice from somewhere in the distance. Great. All I needed was to add *humans* to the mix. Other than me, of course.

I dodged what I could only assume was one of the several fists the creature charging me had and rolled away. It was either a fist or a deformed knee. Its anatomy was unclear. But either way, it broke through the plastic liner inside the subway car, then smashed a hole in the wall and bent the metal frame. It tried to yank it out while all seven of its other arms, or legs, or whatever they were, were currently tangled up by Splinter, who had found some trip-wire in one of my many pockets and went to work being a nuisance to bad guys. Every time the creature that looked like the unholy progeny of a spider and a warthog tried to stand, Splinter wound around the dominant foot and tripped it again.

"Shit," I muttered when I counted a ninth arm. "I really hate this thing."

I calmly raised my boot, flipped the switch on the heel with my other foot, and aimed. Thirty tiny poison-laced spikes protruded from the bottom, and I slammed it directly into where I figured a vital organ had to be. I expected resistance. There was none. Instead, whatever I hit was a soft spot, and my leg went into the creature at full speed, nearly tripping me.

To make matters worse, it flailed and kicked its other legs and sent Splinter careening to the other side of the car with the tripwire, which wrapped around my free foot. I reached for a standing handle and barely managed to wrap my fingers around it to stop me from sliding into the goo that now took up most of the floor. It was disgusting. More disgusting than the average Chicago subway, at least.

Maybe it was more of a squid than an octopus.

I had hopped on the subway line to get to Addison, a short walk from Wrigley Field, where I could catch up with Ally and Archie and maybe have a shot at some pizza. But no. I got on the one fricking subway with an entire group of Farsiders, either by their plan or dumb Sara Slick luck and now I'd be fortunate to survive. I hung onto the handle and reached inside my jacket for the communicator, then pressed the button and shoved it into my ear. Archie had modified an old Bluetooth headset for me, but since I thought people who wore those all the time looked like douches, mine tended to stay in my pocket.

"Archie." I tried to slide my feet under me enough to get both hands back on the handle. It didn't work well. "I might need some help, guys."

A muffled sound came through the headset and Ally's voice broke through.

"Umm, maybe not right this second, Slick."

"Ally, what's going on? I have a tram full of Farsiders, and I need your help."

"Well, everything's fine. Just fine. We have a bit of a—"

"A freaking crisis, that's what!" Archie shouted in the background. It also sounded like he was in the process of whacking something.

"Can you handle it?" Ally prompted.

"Yes." I finally gained some traction under my feet. "Still planning to meet me on Addison?"

A sound like a blowhorn filled my ear, and I squinted.

"Now I am," Archie confirmed. "We might be a little way away, but I'm sure you'll find us. Can't miss us, in fact. Don't forget the new runes, Slick! It's Archie, by the way."

I sighed. No matter how many times we used an intercom system, Archie still felt the need to let me know that the only male voice I heard was him. I didn't have time to ask why I wouldn't be able to miss them, but I assumed whatever he was batting was making a scene.

"Got it," I replied, but a blood-curdling scream in the next car over cut me off. I swiveled my head in that direction and could barely see what looked like an orange-shaded blur scurrying away from something with fangs. It took a second to realize the orange blur was a woman's hair as she dove away from what was most certainly a low-level bloodsucker. "Vampires. Gotta go," I yelled, and snapped the communicator out of my ear. So much for their help.

I swung on the handlebar while hoping it would handle my full weight and shot my feet out. I kicked the back of my right foot and brought the spikes back inside the boot in mid-air, then gracefully landed after the gooey mess that used to be a Farsider.

Splinter ran up my leg and settled on my shoulder, then hid in my hair. The tripwire he used, now covered in goop, was undoubtedly in one of my many pockets. I reached in one and found a long, smooth piece of bone and pulled it out.

It was one of Archie's latest attempts at creating a rune from vampire bones. I had been able to bring him several pieces of them from earlier run-ins, but any time Archie tried to make anything with them, the result was a blunt instrument with no magic imbued at all. However, he was positive this one would work if I used it against another vampire. Since the bone itself was similar magic, it would allow me to steal their strength, and perhaps use it for myself.

At least, that was his theory.

It vibrated in my hand, a good indication that I was near something it could use. I stalked to the next car and smashed the button. When the doors slid open, two things happened simultaneously. The bone shook so hard it felt like it would vibrate my arm off, and two vampires, a cyclops, and a gremlin stopped what they were doing and stared at me.

They were apparently preparing the orange-headed lady for a meal, and my appearance gave her the chance to scurry toward me.

"Help me!" she yelled as she went past my legs. The cyclops tried to stand to his full height but the eight-foot clearance in the car's center limited him. The gremlin, only three feet tall and with no such problem, simply bared his teeth and hissed. His hundreds of tiny, impossibly sharp teeth managed to gleam in the flat, oppressive subway light.

"Lady, whatever you do, don't move," I muttered to the cowering woman who now hid behind an overturned handicapped seat. "As for you guys, I think this is your last stop."

I charged headlong at them. The gremlin ran at me, teeth first. I activated the shoe again and spiked him right in the face. He rolled away, but I knew he'd be back. Those little fuckers were hard to put down for good.

The cyclops stood where he was, but the vampires went around him on either side. I flicked my wrist and twirled the bone, which now shook so hard I was positive it would come out of my hands. Like it was drawn to them, the bone flew on its own. I barely held on as it contacted one of their chins, then spun the other direction to smash the other in the chest.

A wheezing sound came from the second vampire as he stumbled backward into a seat while the jaw-jacked one checked his mouth.

He looked down into his hand, then back at me. Blood covered his mouth, and one of his fangs now sat in his palm. A bellow of anger welled up, and he charged again. This time, the bone seemed to listen to me rather than do its own thing, and I swung it up to uppercut him in the jaw. Rather than knock him backward, it split his head like a melon, and his body continued forward while blood splattered the inside of the car.

"Oh, gross," I complained while Orange Woman screamed behind me. I swiveled to look at the other vampire and spun the bone in my hand while it hummed. "Ok, dingus, your turn."

Before he could react, a piercing, sharp pain filled my leg, and I looked down to see the gremlin take a chunk out of my shin with his gnashing teeth. I picked up my foot to shake it away, but he hung on and swung with me like an angry, dedicated subway beaver.

Splinter suddenly appeared in mid-air behind him. He landed on the gremlin, and they rolled out of view behind the cyclops that now walked toward me with his hand raised.

I ducked as the enormous fist parted my hair and made a crunching, squishing sound behind me. I rolled off to the side and turned to see the massive cyclops, his one brow furrowed in confusion, shaking his arm to get the impaled body of the second vampire off it. I thought fast and reached into my pocket to find the other rune Archie whipped up for me. I yanked it out, twisted the tube of the lipstick, and smashed the acidic waxy substance on the floor while rolling to make a circle around the giant. He noticed me as I completed the oval and reached down for me. There was a loud metallic creak and he stopped to look down as his body started to sink.

"Bye-bye." I waved. A metal-on-metal crash filled the air, and the cyclops dipped from view as the entire floor area I had encircled fell away, and him with it. I heard several thuds as he tried to raise his head, only to be smashed by the speeding train.

I spun to find the gremlin and caught it in time to see it and Splinter tumble through the open hole.

"Splinter!" I cried and dove toward the opening. For a moment, there was nothing but the passing track. Then, against the wind, and with considerable effort, Splinter's hand reached from the bottom of the train and grasped my finger. I pulled him to safety and breathed a sigh of relief.

"Good job, little guy."

Lights flickered above me, and I realized we must be near the stop, but the train wasn't slowing. It felt like it was gaining speed. I turned toward the next car ahead of me and noticed it was the front cab. I made out the shape of the motorman. He was slumped over with his hand dangling away from the controls and dripping.

"Ah, shit."

I hopped to my feet and tried to open the cab door. It wouldn't budge, likely a victim of post-9/11 security. I cursed a few times as I banged it with the now-ineffective bone rune. I frantically looked around for another way in, then it dawned on me. The only way inside the cab was through the window on the outside. Which meant climbing out of a moving train in a subway.

"You stay here, Splinter. If anyone comes in here after me, you bite the shit out of them, got it?" He nodded, and I turned toward one of the doors. *Here goes nothing.*

I jammed the bone into the seam between the two doors and wedged them apart. Once they separated a few inches, they snapped open all the way, and I had to grab the frame to keep from tumbling out. The wall was close, but it looked like I had a few feet of clearance to wiggle out there. A few metal pieces at about foot height looked like they would carry me over to the front window, where I could smash it open and get inside. I tried not to think about it too much, or I would freak myself out, and instead drew a deep breath and stuck my foot out for the first step.

A few panicked seconds of searching finally got me to my first foothold, and I gingerly stepped onto it. The next was only a foot or two away, and I carefully managed to get my front foot to it while hanging onto the very few crevasses available to me to make it across. Only a few steps stood between me and the window, but I felt the whoosh of the hard brick wall inches behind my back. One slip-up and I would smash into that, then back into the train, and likely under it to join the mangled bodies of the cyclops and the gremlin.

I shut my eyes and tried to shake off the image. There was no time for panic. I had to get to the front, or else I would end up crushed like a tin can anyway. Plus, Splinter would get hurt, and I simply couldn't stand for that.

I stepped to the next foothold and noticed there wasn't

another before the glass. My only option was to jam my foot into the space between the two cabs and hope for the best. It would require me essentially pulling myself onto my side while on a moving train. I didn't give myself time to second guess as I shoved my foot into the crevice and pulled myself up. I could see, upside down, into the cab. The motorman sat crumpled in his seat with blood streaming from his neck and his body grey and lifeless. I reached into my pocket, pulled out my trusty switchblade, and brought it down hard on the glass. It sank inward, leaving a spiderweb of broken glass holding itself together with a wisp of integrity. A simple whack would open it fully, and I could climb inside.

A sound filled the air around me, and I looked up. In the far distance, I saw another tram stopped in our way. People ran away from it, and there were other shapes too. Huge shapes. I had to stop this train, and fast, or else we would all end up dead. I slid inside, wiggled my foot free, and gave myself a hundred tiny glass cuts on parts of my body that I was positive I wouldn't notice until I was in the shower—if I survived.

I landed hard on my back in the tiny cab. I quickly stood, pushed the carcass of the motorman away, and looked at the controls. I had only seconds to act, and there was no foot brake. I could only guess, and hope it worked. A lever in front of me was all the way forward. I shrugged.

I grabbed it with both hands and pulled back hard. The skidding sound of brakes screamed through the air, and I slammed against the control panel. The dead motorman's body soared above me, flew out of the tram, and splatted into the back of the one ahead of us. A crunching, thumping sound suddenly rang through my ears at deaf-ening decibels, and everything stopped.

I tentatively peeked above the controls to look out the smashed front window. The mangled body of the motorman was embedded in the back of the train ahead, mere inches away.

CHAPTER TWO

Splinter's frantic voice brought me out of my shock, and I turned to see him peeking through the broken glass. He was screeching for all he was worth and gesticulating toward something outside the train. I shook the cobwebs off and stood, noting an extraordinarily painful bruise on my right thigh from when I engaged the train's brakes and wondered how well that would go with the broken glass shower later.

I wrestled open the door into the first cab and ran to the already-open door on the side. Splinter yelled wildly from my left, and I looked up to find him scurrying on the top of the car, then running back to gesture at the stop.

"What is going on with you, Splinter? We stopped the tr —" I began while following his gaze to the terminal where the train in front of us had stopped. People were running everywhere, but that was no big shock. People were panicky and stupid, and there was almost a crash. Of course, they would run around.

Then I saw some of the Farsiders. Ah, yeah, okay, that

would do it. Farsiders out in the open freaked humans the freak out. *Makes total sense.* Guess I needed to take care of those stupid Farsiders and might want to keep away from that lion.

Wait.

I don't know how long I stood there staring fixedly at the lion, two monkeys, and a fucking ostrich that were running amok, but by the time I realized I hadn't moved in a while, my jaw hurt from being open so long, and I felt like I desperately needed a drink. Maybe for more than one reason.

"Come on," I shouted to the world in general and ran for the area where most people were. Farsiders of varying kinds dotted the crowd and indiscriminately swung, knocked people back and generally wreaked havoc. I had to try to ignore the lion and other animals and focus on the bad guys. As much as possible. I jammed the communicator back in my ear and pressed the button.

"Archie!"

"Saw the lion, didn't you?"

"Archie, what the hell is a lion doing in the subway?"

"Well, not being in the zoo, I know that."

"Archie…"

"Farsiders," Ally's voice broke in. "We decided to go to the zoo while you went off. It was chaos, Slick. Absolute chaos."

"What happened?"

"It was this great beastly thing." Archie's voice crackled in again. He was in full storytelling mode now. "Arms like tree trunks and he had horns coming from his nose. Looked like a rhino on steroids, he did. Anyway, he barreled through the zoo, unlocked cages, and tossed the guards into the pits, and even ripped one guy's arm right off! We booked it for the van, but they were everywhere. I was getting a capuchin out of the passenger seat when you called the first time!"

I was near the crowd now and hopped up onto the platform while sliding under a galloping zebra, who must have noticed that the apex predator was otherwise distracted, and the getting was now extremely good.

"That's great Archie, but why? Why the zoo?"

"Mayhem. That's what they want. Mayhem. And boy, do they have it. The lion dove into the subway entrance after an ostrich when we pulled up. I wouldn't want to be between those two. Dog is somewhere in there trying to corral a few of the more vicious animals, but we lost track of him."

I noticed that most of the people, the regular human people, had cleared out. Now it was only Farsiders. And worse, Harbingers. Little red tattoos on their arms gave them away. The devotees of Hobbes were doing his bidding. What's more, they were armed. Two of them saw me and pulled out crude runes. This would call for the big guns.

My jacket had a secret pocket, deep on my left side, and I slipped my hand in it as I made my way toward them. I found the item inside and slid it over my wrist, then snapped it out and activated it in one motion. A thick stick, which looked impossibly sharp, flew at me and snapped in half. The bracelet had covered me with magical armor, which now made itself visible. It struck me that it looked like it was from the old movie *Tron*. Electric blue and pink lights surrounded me for several feet on all sides. I balled my fist and the armor balled up the mixture of light nearby. I swung and made contact with the human-looking Harbinger, and it was like he got hit by a truck at full speed.

The area went silent as everyone looked at the fallen Farsider. Some of the closest ones hesitated for a moment. They'd seen up close how powerful the shot had been, as well as the burning electric shock that came with it. Suddenly, a roar arose, and multiple Harbingers attacked, some with weapons and others smashing their fists into the wall of nearly faded pink and blue.

Apparently, the electric effect only happened when I attacked. I felt the armor chip away with every blow. Archie had warned me that it might not be a terribly durable item, but it should get me out of a tough jam if I needed it. This certainly qualified.

I kicked forward, smashed another Farsider against a wall, and made my way to the exit steps. I put my head down and opted for brute force to get through the crowd, and Harbingers flew like bowling pins. I was halfway up the stairs when a sharp pain stabbed me in the arm. I looked down to see a trickle of blood.

The armor was fading fast. The lion barreled by me and dove onto a Farsider as he made his way into the sunlight. He was on my side for the moment, but that wouldn't last long. Only a few more steps to the top, then into Archie's RV. Fuck this sticking around stuff. I was outnumbered, out-weaponed, and out-lioned.

I crested the top of the steps and looked around wildly. Archie and the mobile lab were nowhere in sight. I touched the earpiece and noticed I wasn't alone. The street was full of ugly bastards I recognized as being more Farsiders. I stood between them and a huddled mass of humans, many of them hurt.

"Archie, where are you?" I shouted.

"Two blocks away," Ally's voice informed me. "The zoo wasn't the only place broken into. There are people and animals everywhere. Hang tight!"

The Farsiders were already smashing into the armor as they attacked. I tried to swipe them away. I knew it wouldn't last for too much longer, but I had to keep going. These people depended on me as they tried to shuffle away. I had to give them time to escape. My armor would protect me as long as it could, and I was their armor, protecting them.

I set my jaw, bore down, and swiped at a large group of Farsiders, sending them ass-over-teakettle in various directions. I held on for a few more moments and willed the armor to hang on with me. My efforts made a huge dent in Harbingers at street level, but I felt the armor cracking.

I had no idea what would happen when the bracelet failed, but knowing Archie, I knew it wouldn't be clean or simple. Items he made that failed tended to be destructive, including to the user. I closed my eyes and waited. It released.

For a moment, there was nothing. Sound seemed to disappear completely, and I nearly thought I had died. There was no new pain, no fire, no panic in the street—only silence. Then, like the sound of a banshee, a screaming pitch of unholy proportions emanated from the earth itself.

It filled everything, and where sound couldn't be perceived, it sent vibrations. Then an explosion started a foot in front of me and fired out into the crowd of remaining Farsiders. The ones closest were blown apart, limbs flying and landing on parked cars. The ones farthest away were knocked backward a block or so, pushed by a combination of electrical explosiveness and sound waves.

I crumpled to my knees in a combination of pain and a desire to get away from the sound. I covered my ears, but that only seemed to make it worse. I felt the vibrations in my eyes as shockwave after shockwave reverberated out of a small radius with me as the epicenter. The road itself upended in the center of the street, and several of the Harbingers fell into it. It was like hell had opened to swallow them whole.

My hands clawed at the concrete as I let out a scream to match the pain of the vibrations, and I didn't stop until I felt a hand grab me. I turned, ready to fight one last time, to give everything in battle, and stopped when I saw Ally's face.

"Come on, Slick! We gotta go!" she cried. Behind her, Archie stood at the open door of the mobile lab and beckoned me to come to him. I rose on wobbly legs with great relief and ran for the door. As I dove inside, I caught one last glimpse of a man, a human, who had escaped and looked back to see me.

Our eyes met, and he nodded in respect. The door shut before I could respond, and Ally punched the gas and maneuvered the RV around. Splinter, who had made his way into my jacket at some point, scurried out as I raised my head to look out the window. A Harbinger stood in the center of the ruined mass of his brethren and held his arms aloft. I heard him screaming through the chaos.

"We are The Far! We have only begu—," he began but was cut brutally short. A horn impaled him from behind and shoved his body forward as it suddenly danced like a marionette. We turned sharply, and I saw that the horn belonged to a rhino, who now shook its head violently to get him off. The mobile lab careened into an alley, and in seconds we were on a highway, barreling away from the mayhem.

CHAPTER THREE

"I swear, at some point, I'm going to wrap you in bubble wrap before you leave the house," Ally scolded as she cleaned off another cut and covered it with a bandage.

We'd driven a few minutes away from most of the insanity, and were parked at the back of a parking lot piecing ourselves back together.

"That could have some bad implications for my range of motion and mobility," I pointed out. "And unless you wanted me to suffocate, you couldn't wrap my head, so I would still have a lot of vulnerable surface area and nowhere to hobble."

"You always manage to find the bad in even the best plans," she complained.

"You could make me a bubble wrap helmet and use mesh for the face," I offered.

"There you go. That's the spirit."

"All things considered, I think that went pretty well." I admired the newly bandaged injury.

My attempt at optimism didn't seem to brighten the

mood in the mobile lab much. It still didn't have a name, which I felt bad about. But with so much going on plus attempting to save the world and everything, I didn't have a lot of time to think about it. Hopefully, the RV wouldn't hold it against me.

"If you've put Humpty-Dumpty back together again, we should move. We need to get out of the city," Archie advised.

"You made a human reference that made sense. I'm so proud of you," I told him.

"What's going on?" Ally climbed behind the wheel and started the RV again.

"Look at this."

Archie had been watching something on Ally's phone and now propped it on the dashboard so we could all see it. The news playing out on the screen was grim. Strange events and brutal attacks were happening all over the world.

Journalists scrambled to report on the events, but there wasn't much they could say. The truth was, they had no idea what was going on. They couldn't explain the massive assaults from groups wearing masks and hoods. They didn't know what to say about the buildings collapsing or the horrific events that seemed like natural disasters but came without warning or pattern.

"Holy hell," I muttered. "Harbingers everywhere."

"They're attacking without any rhyme or reason. It seems like whoever happens to cross their path gets wiped out," Archie confirmed. "It's not a centralized location anymore. The attacks are spread out across the globe, and there's no way to figure out where they'll target next."

"And the humans haven't come up with any ideas about who it might be?"

Flashes of the almost disastrous peace summit made me think about who people would blame for all that was happening. Someone had to catch the blame for it, and that could quickly go downhill for whoever it was.

"There have been instances of retaliation," Archie admitted.

My eyes snapped to him.

"Retaliation? Who are people retaliating against?"

"Some of the Harbingers left connections to their Farsider communities. Not enough to reveal who and what they are, but enough so humans can attack them back."

"Fantastic," Ally muttered. "I'm sure that's going over well."

"A bunch of pissed-off humans who don't want to be the little boats in a big-ass game of Battleship blasting the hell out of Farsider communities that may or may not have anything to do with the attacks?" I responded. "Yep. Sounds like good times all around. I expect a reunion picnic to break out at any second."

"They're getting aggressive," Archie confirmed. "The communities are acting out and attacking the humans who attacked them. The Harbingers are building up militias among the Farsiders, even those who never wanted animosity between Farsiders and humans. If it was their plan all along to create fights all over the place that will whip up the battles and hasten the war, they're doing an exceptional job."

Ally questioned, "And if it wasn't their plan?"

"Then they're lucky as fuck," I told her.

"Essentially," Archie agreed.

The reporter on the screen kept rambling, saying the same thing over and over without getting anywhere. In a way, that was a good thing.

"There might be some retaliation going on, but it's by pure dumb luck. The humans don't know what's happening," I noted.

"So it seems," Archie agreed.

"That means the Philosophers are still doing their cover-up job. But, honestly, how long can they last? With all this shit happening everywhere, how long can they keep up with excusing everything away?"

"About as long as non-waterproof makeup on a drag queen singing her third song during pageant season," Ally murmured.

I stared at her. Blink. Blink, blink.

"I wish I knew what that meant," I told her flatly. "Genuinely. I wish I had any context at all."

The image on the screen shrank slightly as a call came in. Ally glanced at it and made a worried sound. I looked at the number in the banner across the top of the screen. My eyes shot to Ally, but she was suddenly extremely invested in paying attention to the road in front of her. The phone kept ringing as I looked at Archie. He was already shaking his head. No help there. Dog had curled up on the floor, so I didn't bother looking at him. I was apparently on my own.

I snatched the phone out of its holder and answered it.

"Hi, Senator." I hoped I sounded breezy and not possessed.

There was kind of a fine line there, and I wasn't always the best at staying on the right side of it.

"What in the living hell is going on?" Senator Cabot demanded.

I cringed, and Ally pulled off. This was going to be one of those conversations that required more than me. At least we had made it out of the city and were now on the outskirts. It was quieter, and I felt less like any second we would end up as extras in a seriously messed up PETA PSA.

"This is the opening salvo." I tried my best to explain what was going on. "Hobbes is done acting in the shadows. He's finally going all out to destabilize the *Pax* and lead to war."

"What's next?" she asked.

I looked at Archie, who was still shaking his head. I sighed.

"All hell breaks loose."

Cabot fell silent on the other end. I tried to picture her face.

"I've been doing what I can, keeping people calm. But it can't last."

"I know," I agreed. "We have to do something."

"What?" Desperation crept through her voice.

"I don't know. We're still in the brainstorming phase of that, and waiting for an epiphany. Or a guidebook of some kind. This isn't like anything we've ever dealt with. Wait."

"How do you plan to handle this?" the senator prompted. "Is there anyone who can help us?"

I tried to think if there was anyone out there who could help us. Pip was busy dealing with some problems among the Lizard People. After our last adventure together, she had gone back home to see if the Harbingers were making any ground with her people. The Dryads might be able to help, but their M.O. was to keep low, which was probably the safest option right now. The last thing we needed was an Entmoot on the evening news.

I was opening my mouth, hoping something useful would come out, when there was a knock at the door.

"Perfect," I grumbled. "Just what we need right now. The police coming to hassle us because we're out in the middle of nowhere. Let's wager on which of us they'll accuse of being the prostitute this time."

"Me," Archie said without hesitation.

The senator's involuntary snort momentarily lightened my spirits as I ended the call, then plastered on my best we're-only-a-bunch-of-humans-not-doing-anything-suspicious smile and opened the door. That smile dropped from my face when I saw Bentham standing outside.

CHAPTER FOUR

"Fuck!" I yelled and slammed the door. Unfortunately for me, she stepped closer and pulled on it, trying to force it open. I pulled the opposite way. We struggled with it, one on either side, while the rest of my group looked on in confusion.

"Stop it, Slick," Bentham called through grunts of effort.

"You stop it," I yelled back. "Archie, for God's sake, hit the gas, will you?"

"Stop holding the damn door! I need to talk to you."

She gave one final hard yank and pulled me off balance. I let go and stumbled back so I didn't take a header, and Bentham entered the lab. Archie and Ally jumped up, and Dog got to his feet while growling.

"Get out of here, Bentham," I hissed.

Without any of my weapons at close range, my only option was to lunge at her. The small space didn't work to my advantage as much as I hoped it would. She easily saw me coming and stepped out of my way by ducking over toward the couch, then moved toward the back of the RV.

"Wait. We need to talk."

"Fuck talking," I shouted. "You and your partner tried to kill me with a giant axe."

She avoided another lunge by moving behind a stack of milk crates Archie collected for reasons that were still unclear to me. They toppled forward, hitting me and piling at my feet so I couldn't move toward her.

"You took the axe and killed other people with it," Bentham pointed out.

"Well, I didn't say I forgave you. And I definitely didn't tell you I had any interest in being in the same space with you ever again."

"Nothing you can do about that," she countered. "I'm already here, and you need to listen to me."

"Like hell she does." Archie and Ally came up behind me, but I held up my hand. "No. Leave her. She's mine."

The fallen crates cluttered the entire space across the RV, which forced me to kick my way through them.

"Are you kidding me?" Bentham asked.

"I've always wanted to say that." I finally pushed enough of the crates out of the way to get through them. "I figure there's a lot of shit going down and I might miss my opportunity, so I'm going to use it on you. Now get over here so I can throw you out."

I scrambled toward her, and Bentham held up a hand.

"I will make you listen if I have to."

"I need to get you out of my face so I can keep doing what needs doing."

Her hand glowed with powerful magic, but I ducked in time for it to sail over my head. If she was going to arrest me, she would have to work for it. I rolled right and ended up behind a crate that blocked another blast. It was surprisingly weak.

Bentham's usual magical shots should have made kindling out of the wooden crate, but this one only put a hole in it. Obviously, her orders were to bring me in unhurt, probably so her boss could do it herself.

I kicked the crate hard and low and sent it tumbling toward her. It hit her directly in the chin before she could move and she went down hard on her back. I jumped to my feet and landed a hard kick to her ribs that rolled her away. She didn't fall exactly the way I hoped she would. I'd envisioned she'd land flat on her face, and I could yank her arms around behind her, pin her down with my knee, and drag her out of the mobile lab.

I looked forward to tossing her out on the side of the road and having Ally drive off. Maybe we could pull off the tires squealing and spinning to spit a bunch of dust and gravel right in the agent's face. It would have been epic.

Unfortunately, it didn't work out like that. Instead, Bentham turned enough to fling her arm out and grab me by the leg, which threw me off balance. We both hit Archie's lab counter.

"Not my lab!" he shouted in vain as some of the bottles and containers toppled over.

"I won't break anything else if she'll calm down and listen," Bentham grumbled loudly. I responded by kicking her in the hip. She tumbled over, and we both made it to our feet at the same time. Her hand extended, fingers glowing with another spell. My hand was up too, now brandishing a broken glass bottle. It wasn't the world's most elegant weapon, but it would do a number on her nose if I got close enough.

"Calm down, Slick."

"Calm down?" I shouted incredulously. "You want me to calm down? Haven't you paid attention to what's going on out there? Humans are fucking dying right and left. The Harbingers are decimating whole towns. They're destroying lives, and you're out here trying to arrest me. The world is in complete chaos, and you want me to calm down? Sounds like a great idea. Maybe I'll kick back and knit myself a pair of footie pajamas so I can settle in for winter."

She lunged, and I dodged, caught her hand, and swept her in one motion. I locked the armbar and jammed my knee into her back as she crashed to the floor of the RV. She started to say something else, but I crushed my forearm against the back of her neck. Bentham struggled against me. She was bigger than I was and was a trained and skilled fighter.

I'd spent ten years rotting away in prison, but even if I'd stayed free and clear and had joined a gym to work on my biceps, she would still be more physically imposing. She almost struggled away from me, and I pressed all my weight into my knee and forearm, and she stopped.

"This would be the time where I could use some help," I called to the others at the front of the RV.

"I thought we were supposed to stand back," Archie reminded me.

"She's yours and all that," Ally added.

"This isn't the time for the two of you to be smartasses. Especially since something is dripping off Archie's counter and it's getting disturbingly close to my eye," I retorted. Dog growled again and came toward us, but I shook my head. At least, as much as I could while still holding Bentham down. "No. Don't you dare. Not while I'm holding onto her. I won't have you miss and take half my face off."

Archie ran forward and pushed the crates away to get to us, then reached down and grabbed Bentham. Ally came up behind him, and together they wrenched at her as I released my knee. I kept my arm latched over her neck to hold her still. They tugged, but I didn't release her.

"Slick, you need to let go," Archie pointed out. "We can't get her up if you're still holding her head down."

"I'll keep her head. You can take the rest of her." I gave her head a sharp yank back against me.

Bentham made a gargling sound, and her teeth scraped against my arm.

"Let go," Archie repeated.

I reluctantly released the agent, and he pulled her up, then dragged her over to the couch. As he did, Dog snapped at her. It was more to scare her than anything. If he had wanted to get her with his vicious teeth, he would have.

I jumped to my feet and reached over the counter to where my switchblade sat. Archie had been playing with it, but now I needed it back. I crossed the RV and descended on Bentham, my blade pulled back in preparation. Her eyes widened, and she put one arm up, not to fight, but in defense.

"I'm not here to arrest you, dammit!" she yelled.

"Slick, stop!" Ally demanded. "Put it away."

"No. She got away from me before. I won't let that happen again."

Dog growled and snarled behind me. Although I'd never seen him eat anyone, this might be the time he tried. With the horrific attacks going on around us, the thought of releasing one of the people probably responsible for them wasn't on either of our minds.

"Calm down," Ally ordered. "Maybe we should let her talk for a minute. She hasn't tried to kill you since she got here. You could at least extend her the same courtesy."

"It disturbs me that you now consider that courtesy. I've ruined you."

"I would believe your indignation better if you weren't holding a knife to someone's throat right now. Give it to me." She reached for my weapon, but I moved so I blocked her and prevented her from snatching it from me. "Seriously. Give it to me and calm down. No need to get blood in here. More of it, at least."

I looked at Ally. She stared into my eyes until I finally relented.

"Fine. But I won't let her loose. Not until I know what's going on."

Splinter suddenly burst out of his cabinet and launched himself at Bentham. He scrambled all over her, nipping and biting as he went, but never stayed in one place long enough for her to swat him away.

"Stop him!" Bentham demanded.

I gave him another second before I grabbed him by one of his arms and picked him up. He continued to flail and gnash his teeth for a moment, then realized he wasn't doing anything productive and stopped.

"Thank you for coming to my defense, Splinter. You're as valiant as you are handsome."

He leapt toward Ally, obviously hoping for a beautiful moment where she would catch him, and they would spin together in slow motion, but it didn't work out for him. She caught him, but it was at arms' length, and she quickly deposited him on Dog's back.

"Now will you let me talk?" Bentham asked.

"Yes. What the hell is going on here? Your new technique is to knock on our door?"

"Not a new technique, a new mission. I'm not here to arrest you, Slick."

"Then why are you here?"

She sighed. "I came here for your help."

It sounded almost as painful and awkward for her to say as it was to hear.

"Excuse me, what?"

"I came for your help," she repeated, which confirmed that I heard her correctly.

"Why?"

"You're the only one to ever break out of The Deep."

"Yeah? So?"

"So, who better to help me break into The Heights than you?"

CHAPTER FIVE

"You really think this is necessary?" Bentham asked.

Archie took another bungee cord from the emergency kit and wrapped it tightly around her. She was bound to a chair with her ankles knotted together and anchored to the support legs on either side, and her thighs fastened to the seat. More cords restrained her hips, waist, and chest, and he'd tied her hands at the wrist.

"Yes," I told her. "I think it's essential. You haven't exactly proven yourself trustworthy in the past. I won't get caught with my ass out because you came in here all dramatic and we had an Oprah moment. I'm willing to listen to what you have to say, as long as you're willing to be properly restrained while you say it. The alternative is we throw you out of the moving vehicle."

Archie yanked on the final cord to make sure it was tight.

"Satisfied?" Bentham asked.

"Go ahead," I told her.

"Are you positive? You don't need to put the crates over

my head or pile a couple of stones in my lap for good measure?" she asked.

"Do you want me to put Splinter down your shirt?"

I glanced over at the strange little creature. He looked thrilled to be called a weapon and a threat.

"No. I've had enough of him for now."

"Good. Then why don't you tell me what's going on?"

"Things are getting strange in The Heights," Bentham started. "It's well known the attacks on the humans are coming from Hobbes and the Harbingers."

"It doesn't take a tremendous leap of the imagination to come to that conclusion," Ally commented from where she sat on the couch.

"What's the Guild going to do about it?" I asked. "This is as much their problem as it is a problem for humans. If they don't get this under control fast, Hobbes will have his way, and soon the world will crack open like a Cadbury creme egg."

"I don't know what that means," Bentham told me.

"It will be messy."

"Yes. Extremely. If this continues and Hobbes gets what he wants, it will undo the *Pax,* and there will be mass destruction," Bentham confirmed.

"So, what are they doing about it?" I asked.

Bentham sighed. "Not enough. We have our agents out, doing their best to keep the peace. But obviously, this is more than our standard agents can handle. And instead of helping, every high-level Guild Agent has been pulled from containment. Rand doesn't want us concentrating on taking down Harbingers or protecting humans or preserving the *Pax.* We have one mission. Take you down."

"Me?" I looked from Bentham to Archie and Ally. "What the shit?"

"What the shit, indeed. I questioned it. Rand immediately reprimanded me, but it didn't sit right. I couldn't ignore that feeling and do as instructed. So, I rebelled."

"What do you mean, you rebelled?" Archie asked.

Bentham gave him a look I could only describe as distasteful. There was some history there, and it wasn't the fun kind that translated into a summer rom-com romp. It was more a simmering, bitter tension.

"We were sent to Chicago. You were spotted here. Nobody knew why or what you were doing, but it didn't matter. You were here, so that's where our leadership directed us. The orders were to find and destroy you."

"That's pleasant," I interjected.

"But when I saw the Harbinger chaos firsthand, I wanted to help. It was too much. I told Thrash what I was thinking, and asked him to come with me, to do something good for once. He said our orders were to ignore the other humans, but I refused.

"I wasn't going to stand by and allow this horrific violence to happen when there was something I could do about it. So, I did what I could. I saved a large group of people from rampaging centaurs, but when I wanted to do more, it went bad. Thrash and the other Guild Agents turned on me. Which is when I learned what kind of person my partner was."

"He was reporting back to Rand."

She nodded. "How did you know?"

"I learned to read the room really well when I was in

The Deep. He struck me as a snitch from the very beginning."

Bentham nodded again. "He told me Rand knew I would go rogue and had no belief in my commitment to the Guild or my responsibilities within it. She ordered him to keep an eye on me and make sure I was doing what she meant to do. And nothing else. He instantly reported me, took the key that allows me to travel between realms, and prepared to send me to Rand for judgment. But I escaped."

"How did you do that?" Ally asked.

"Because she's a badass." Bentham looked at me in surprise, and I didn't take my eyes away from her. "I don't like you, and I think the people you work for are scum, but I can appreciate and admire your skills. You nearly kicked my ass on several occasions and gave me a run for my money in here. I had to call for help to take you down. Of course, a lot of that had to do with the unidentified mystery liquid from Archie's lab."

"What color was it?" Archie asked.

"Green."

"Were there any flecks in it? Did it smoke?"

"No."

"Jell-O," he said matter-of-factly.

"Excuse me?"

"Lime, to be exact. I recently discovered drinking it. I like to mix it with the boiling water, add the cold water really slowly, then drink it down and pretend it turns solid in my belly."

"You're alone in this van for far too long sometimes, aren't you?"

"Yes."

There was no argument, no attempt at justification—only a simple acknowledgment.

"Anyway," Bentham continued, "I escaped. And since my tally of friends is now zero, there was nothing left but to turn to an enemy. Something rotten is happening within the Guild and has somehow compromised it and Rand. I may not like you, but I know that you've been a major thorn in the Harbingers' side since you escaped.

"You deserve to rot in The Deep, but Rand's orders to focus on you now benefits no one but Hobbes, so she's either on his payroll, or she's an idiot. And she's no idiot. I don't know what her game is, but the only place to find the truth is in The Heights. That's the only place where I'll get answers and be able to do anything beneficial. But I can't do it on my own. They took my key, and they'll have Agents out everywhere, combing existence for me. I need help from someone who knows how to get out of impossible places. Only this time, I need your help getting into one." Bentham half-laughed.

"If the Guild is compromised…" Ally whispered.

"Then it means Hobbes could have been in The Heights this whole time," I pointed out.

Archie nodded. "It would make sense. That would explain why we haven't been able to find him. If he's in The Heights, he's fully protected."

"Not fully," Bentham countered. "Not if I can get back in there."

I drew in a breath and held it, hoping it might help me figure something out. When it didn't, I let it out in a gush. I had no idea what I should do.

CHAPTER SIX

"I need to think about this," I said. "It's a lot coming at me right now. I'm going to step outside for a minute."

Bentham nodded. "Untie me, and I'll go with you. We'll talk it out."

I scoffed at her. "Hell, no. Smooth try, there, but I'm the one they call Slick. You'll keep your Guild-y little ass right there in that chair while *I* go outside to think. Archie, make sure she stays tied up. Don't believe her if she says it's too tight and wants you to loosen it. Dog, watch her. If she moves, rip her throat out. Splinter, you watch her, too. If she moves," I tilted my head to look directly into his little beady eyes, "do worse."

Splinter hopped onto Dog's back again, and they took their position directly in front of Bentham. Dog probably didn't love that my little franken-rodent used him as a personal transportation device, but he didn't protest.

Bentham eyed them both and pulled back slightly against the chair like she was trying to get as far away from them as possible. I snatched my leather jacket from where it was draped over the back of one of the seats and shrugged into it as I walked out of the mobile lab.

I wished I could have stood there and taken deep breaths of fresh, cleansing night air to clear my mind and help me process, but it was only so fresh this close to the highway. At least I wasn't inside the vehicle anymore and could see the sky. For what it was worth, the air was cooler and helped to settle me down a little. I walked several paces away from the RV into the shadows and crossed my arms over my chest.

The door slammed, and I looked up to see Ally coming toward me. She was tugging Archie's sweater close around her. This wasn't the first time I noticed her being rather familiar with Archie and his oversized hoodies and sweaters. She walked toward me without talking, waiting for me to be the one to start the conversation.

Looking at my best friend standing there, fresh injuries wrapped in bandages, signs of others still apparent on her skin, made everything press down on me even harder. She had given up everything for me without question, without hesitation. When everybody else pushed thoughts of me aside and gave me up as dead, Ally didn't. She wouldn't let go and wouldn't simply move on without me.

Then, after ten years of being gone, I showed back up in her life, and she was willing to jump in. By all rights, she could have told me I was insane and run away as fast as she possibly could in the opposite direction. It would have been totally understandable. Instead, she followed me. She filled me with tacos and fought right alongside me. She was still here, walking around on the outskirts of Chicago with the image of a man getting trampled by a rhino fresh in her mind, and wasn't trying to leave me behind.

It made me want to push even harder to justify her loyalty, but it also made me hesitate. What was in front of us was far more than we'd encountered so far, and it would only get more intense. It wasn't only about Ally. It was Archie and Dog and Splinter—and me.

"Should I do this?" I finally asked.

"Did I really hear what I think I heard?" Ally joked and walked closer. "Does the great Sara Slick doubt herself?"

"Not myself. The situation. You have to admit that this is some twisted stuff. How many times have we had run-ins with Bentham and her dear friend Sir Smashalot? She's always been Guild to the core. If she had her way, I'd have been dead a long time ago, or at least shoved back into The Deep, which would have been worse. But now she shows up at our mobile lab asking for help? I don't know if I can trust her." I kicked the ground for a moment and sighed.

"Well, like you said, she's almost always been with Thrash. Except for that one awkward music festival incident, we always see her with him," Ally noted.

"So?" I grunted.

"So, he's not here this time. She showed up on her own without any backup or an enforcer to talk to you. She didn't use magic to fight you off when she could have. You were in there flailing around like a madwoman, and she ran away from you. That doesn't sound like she came here to take you down," she pointed out.

"What do you think about her story?"

Ally shrugged. "I don't know. Why would the Guild know the world was on the brink of war because of these

Harbinger attacks, but instead of trying to deal with them, send their top people after you?"

I sighed again. "Remember the book? The one about Hobbes? I'm smeared all over that thing. They think I'm this heinous creature who did all these terrible things. Now that the timing works out so nicely that I get out and the whole world goes to hell, they might think I could have something to do with it."

"Do you think they could suspect you of being responsible for this?" Ally wondered.

"I don't know what they think. But if Rand is sending all her people after me, I'm in some serious trouble."

"Unless Bentham really did rebel and went rogue to come and find you for help."

As if that sentence was a cue of some kind, the quiet exploded in shouts. My head snapped in the direction of the lab in time to see a swarm of Guild Agents coming toward us.

There were at least a dozen of them, probably more, and they poured over the mobile lab and onto the shoulder of the highway where Ally and I stood. The world went white as a blast of cold magic exploded into the ground a foot from Ally. She dove out of the way, and I instinctively moved into her vacant place. She rolled until she was under the mobile lab. One of the Agents was already on me.

He swung a roundhouse punch, but I ducked, struck him twice in the stomach with my fist, then jumped forward to smash his nose with the top of my head. He fell backward, unconscious, as another agent attacked me from behind. A blast of red-tinted magic, which felt hot and smelled like burnt tires, barely missed my shoulder.

I struggled with the attacking agent until I wrestled him to the ground, and we jockeyed for position. Our momentum kept us rolling, and out of the corner of my eye, I saw another aim his hand at us to cast another magical blast. I relented and allowed the one I fought to gain the upper hand in time for him to take the full measure of the shot on his back. He fell forward on top of me as smoke billowed from his eyes and a trickle of blood trailed from his nostrils.

These Agents weren't fucking around.

The door of the lab opened, and Dog bounded out. He dove on one of the Agents and tore into him while Ally jumped into the RV behind him. I ran to follow her, but another agent came between us. He went for the door, and I grabbed him by the back of his neck, then spun him around.

I smashed my foot into his kneecap and heard it snap, which made him kneel toward it. As he did, I slammed my knee into his jaw and shoved him to the ground. Another magical blast missed me, but singed my hair and landed on the side of the RV, where it burned a hole in the siding. I dove inside, and Dog leapt in behind me.

"We gotta move," Archie screamed. I slammed the door shut, and the vehicle lurched to life as I turned back to Bentham with hatred flowing through my veins.

CHAPTER SEVEN

Archie wasn't a good driver. It was a safe assumption before, but now that I was in the back of the RV careening down the highway with him behind the wheel, it was a certainty.

He wove all over the place, jerking the steering wheel back and forth to sling the vehicle across the lanes. I was incredibly thankful it wasn't the middle of the day, and he wasn't wiping other people out along the way. Ally pulled herself up off the floor where she'd fallen when Archie launched us forward. She clawed toward the front and grabbed the wheel.

"Get the hell out of the way," she demanded. "We're trying not to die right now."

Archie wriggled out of the way, and Ally took over, then straightened us out and regained control. I turned on Bentham and seethed.

"It was a trap!" I shouted. "You set us up! I knew I couldn't trust you."

"Slick, listen to me," Bentham begged.

"Oh, shit!" Ally shouted.

She yanked on the steering wheel and wrenched us to the side so hard I was positive we would roll over at any second. As we spun, a massive explosion destroyed the section of road where we were just traveling. A blast of fire shot across it and created a wall of flames in front of us.

"They're using magic," Bentham advised. "There's nothing you can do."

"Fuck that," Ally scoffed. "You think we'll stop and let them nuke us because of a little explosion?"

"That's exactly what she wants," I told her, then descended on Bentham again. "That was the plan all along. She came here pretending to be a refugee from the Guild, asking for my help for some bullshit mission to The Heights. All she did was stall us so the Agents could find us. If you stop, they'll get to us."

"That's not what's happening," Bentham insisted.

"Hold on tight," Ally directed. "We're about to see how the mobile lab reacts to fire."

"Probably not well," Archie cautioned. "I never got around to switching its fuel system."

"We'll find out."

She stomped on the gas, and the RV lurched ahead. I tumbled to the side but managed to catch myself and pull back up to face Bentham.

"You're lucky Ally took my switchblade and put it somewhere. If she hadn't, I'd slit your throat and use you as a battle flag."

"Here we go," Ally announced.

I looked through the window on the side of the vehicle and saw flames surround us. When I switched my gaze to the windshield, I couldn't see anything in front of us but more fire.

"How far is it?"

"I don't know," Ally told me. "I can't see anything ahead."

I leaned menacingly toward Bentham and demanded, "Fix it."

"I can't fix it. What do you want me to do? Throw a water bottle at it?"

"You have magic. De-magic it. Un-magic it. Re-magic it. You pick the fucking prefix and do it."

"I can't simply stop the magic of another agent. That's not how it works."

"What's next? You know the plan. What will they do next?"

"I don't know the plan!" she insisted. "This isn't a trap. Think of it this way, Slick. If it is, it's the stupidest fucking one that ever existed because I'll die with you."

"It wouldn't be the first time someone was willing to lay down their life for something they believe in," I pointed out.

"Except I don't believe in what the Guild is doing! I wouldn't lay down my life for this. I want to stop the Harbingers, not make it easier for them."

"It's getting seriously hot in here," Archie broke in.

"If the gas tank doesn't explode first, the tires will melt," Ally informed him.

"If this isn't a trap, they followed you here," I told Bentham. "They knew you were coming."

"Either that or they already knew where you were because you make a scene wherever you go," Bentham retorted. "How do you know they didn't simply track you and your flailing?"

"Road ahead," Ally announced. "We're almost there."

We watched and held our breath until the RV burst through the other side of the fire.

"They're still behind us," Archie reported. "Slick, here. Take this. It's not done, but it might help."

He handed me what looked like an elaborate peashooter. I glared at him, but grabbed a crate and climbed on it. After grabbing a blanket to protect my hands from the heat, I opened the sunroof Archie had created and popped up out of it. In my mind, I would shoot like an action hero and wipe them all out.

In reality, the rune was finicky and no matter where I aimed, the projectiles didn't go anywhere near the Agents following us as they zoomed in and out of my direct line of sight on motorcycles. I was still impressed they cut right through the fire. The peashooter's ammunition made enough noise and caused sparks that caught the Agents' attention, but unless I wanted to scream *made you look*, that wouldn't be overly beneficial.

"This thing isn't doing anything," I told Archie. "And they're getting closer. At this point, I might be luring them."

"If you don't do something, we're all going to die," Bentham shouted.

She thrashed, and Splinter made a threatening sound at her. I dropped back into the RV and ran to Ally.

"Give me my switchblade."

She nodded at the passenger seat. "It's right there."

I snatched it up and headed back to Bentham. She recoiled as she stared at the knife, then me.

"Seriously? The something you're going to do is kill me?"

"No." I used my blade to slash away the cords and ropes holding her to the chair. "You're going to do something. You can't undo their magic, but you can use yours. If you're really on our side, then prove it."

Without hesitation, Bentham jumped to her feet and climbed up into the hatch. Blasts of magic illuminated the area outside the mobile lab. Archie handed me the peashooter again. I rolled my eyes, but took it and leaned out the window to shoot. This time, I aimed in the opposite direction of where I wanted the projectile to go. While it still didn't go precisely where I wanted it to, there was some contact.

The return attack worked. Bentham's concussive blasts landed and built once, then twice in multiple booming explosions. More than once, the Agents lost control of their bikes and careened off the road. I knew that the blasts she sent were major drains on her energy, but she seemed focused.

More blasts made the majority of the bike-mounted Agents fall back. Finally, they dropped away. I let out a victory cheer an instant before one of the fire-damaged tires blew with a loud popping sound. The RV swerved and tipped as it spun, then crashed through the guard rail on the side of the road. Only it wasn't a road.

It was a bridge.

It was impressive how much profanity I could spew in the time it took for us to tumble through the air and into the river below. We landed with a hard thud and a series of crashes. Then everything went silent.

It took me a few seconds to come to terms with the reality that I could still feel all my body parts. They were still attached where they were supposed to be, and I didn't see an inordinate amount of blood around. Quite a bit of water and mud from the broken windows and open hatch, but not blood.

"Everyone ok?" I asked.

There were enough groans and muttered responses for me to feel confident everyone survived the fall. "There is no way we should have survived that," Archie coughed.

I glanced at Bentham.

"Aethermancy," she replied matter-of-factly. "It protected us inside this thing while we fell."

"You're seriously the fastest magic in the West, aren't you?" I asked.

I looked around and saw Ally and Archie kicking the door of the RV while trying to dig through the mud and water rushing in. "Didn't protect us all the way," Ally groaned. "That wasn't a soft landing."

"I didn't say I floated us down onto a river filled with marshmallows," the agent reminded her.

We climbed out of the mobile lab and made our way to the edge of the riverbank. When I looked around to take in my surroundings, my stomach sank.

"Splinter. Where's Splinter? He can't swim. You remember what happened to him in the ocean!"

Images of him face-down in the water went through my head. Dog walked up to me, having already made it to land, and nudged my leg. I looked down at the soaked, mud-coated animal. He didn't look pleased, but he did look oddly like a chipmunk. I crouched and cupped my hands in front of his face.

He opened his mouth, and Splinter's back end tumbled out. The front was still inside since he clung to Dog's back teeth with his little hands and attempted to pull himself back in. He realized that effort was futile and grabbed onto Dog's lip, then tried to wrap it around himself. I took hold of him, and Splinter started screaming.

"Splinter!" I shouted. "Splinter, it's me, buddy. Let go of Dog."

It took another few seconds of screaming, but he finally complied. I cradled him in my hands and kissed him.

"Did she kiss that thing?" Bentham asked.

"We're working on it," Ally told her.

"They'll never stop me, will they?" I nuzzled Splinter's toilet brush bristles. I leaned down to Dog. "Thank you for letting him hide."

"My lab," Archie suddenly said. I turned to look at him and saw him standing on the edge of the bank while looking at the rubble of what used to be his lab as it slowly sank into the muddy river. "It's destroyed. It's completely totaled."

"I'll help you," Ally soothed. "I'm sure we'll find something we can salvage."

They went to work picking through what was left of the destruction and what they could get from the RV before it completely sank. I went over to Bentham while still cuddling Splinter close to my chest.

"Thank you."

"Don't mention it," she told me.

I drew in a breath and gave a sharp nod. "We're in.

Whatever needs doing, tell me. If it brings down Hobbes, I'll do anything it takes. It's the only way to stop the world from falling apart." Bentham started to answer, but I held up a finger to stop her and made sure she was still listening carefully to what I was saying. "But if you put my friends at risk, I will do something deserving of the word heinous. Do we have an understanding?"

"Yes."

"Good. So, what do we do now?"

CHAPTER EIGHT

"We're too exposed, out here in the open," I noted. "We need to find somewhere to lay low for a while and figure out what we're going to do next."

"There's a highway sign a little way up the road," Archie replied. "Maybe it'll tell us somewhere we can go."

After gathering up everything we could save from the demise of our mobile lab, we climbed up to the highway and walked along the shoulder. I felt on edge with every step. Although I was reasonably certain Bentham's magic forced the Guild Agents back for a while, I still felt like they were watching us. They could spring out of the woods at any second with their magic blazing. We reached the large green sign and saw advertisements for several motel chains off the next exit. But they were all a couple of miles away.

"There's no way we can walk all the way there," Bentham said. "It's too dangerous."

"At this point, the only option we have is to walk," I noted. "Maybe we'll find something else along the way."

The silence pressed in around us as we walked. I heard the whir of distant cars and a few crickets, but that wasn't enough. "Anybody know any good hiking songs? Ally, you were a Girl Scout. Teach us a song."

We were traipsing along and singing about a camel when Archie pointed ahead.

"There's a Welcome Center."

I followed his gesture and sighed. "That's not a Welcome Center, Archie. That's a skeezy gas station with two trailers in back."

"It says 'welcome,'" he pointed out.

"On a piece of cardboard taped above the door," I countered.

"Come on," Ally interjected.

She started toward the cracked parking lot and ominously flickering light next to the door.

"But Alice the camel has no more humps," I reminded her. "We have to finish the song so I can find out what happens."

"I'll tell you in the car."

She jogged away, and the rest of us ran after her.

"The car?" Bentham asked. "I thought you didn't have a car."

"We don't yet. Give me a minute."

Ally brought us into the shadowy back corner of the lot and went around to the driver's side of a burgundy Oldsmobile parked near one of the trailers. She crouched by the door and had it open within seconds. I watched her lean inside and mess with something under the steering wheel.

A few seconds later, the car roared to life. She got to her

feet and grinned at us before gesturing for us all to get inside. We piled in, and she slammed her foot on the gas, rocketing us out of the parking lot before anyone noticed what we were doing.

"I expected lawlessness from Sara Slickerman," Bentham commented. "But your aptitude for criminal activity surprises me, Alejandra. Where did you learn to do that?"

"Ally has lived a couple of different lives," I explained. "And the fate of the world is at stake. A little grand theft auto should be the least of your worries."

"Don't worry," Ally reassured her as we drove toward the nearest motel. "We'll send whoever owns this car a check and a thank you note. Assuming we live long enough. And Slick? Alice is a horse."

"Well, damn."

We drove past a few hotels that seemed too bright and aboveboard for our particular purposes, and eventually made it to a motel so sagging and shitty it felt like home. I smiled as we climbed out of the car and Ally looked at me distastefully.

"Yeah, I figured you'd like it. I'll go rent us a room."

She came back from the lobby a few minutes later with a key card and an ice bucket. We drove around to the back of the motel and went into the room.

"I'm starving," I announced.

"I'll go grab something," Archie replied. "Don't let anyone in the room unless you hear the secret knock. It'll sound like this."

He went over to the door and drummed out a complicated rhythm on it.

"Why don't we simply not let anyone in the room unless we look out through the peephole and see it's you?" I asked.

"You've already forgotten about the shapeshifter, haven't you?"

I shuddered while thinking about how it felt to punch my face. "Good point."

Ally and Bentham sat on the tacky floral bedspreads and watched a black-and-white rerun on a TV that very well could be older than me. When Archie finally returned, it was with a giant bag of tacos and enough guacamole to feed that camel-pretending Alice. Or me, if I'm supplied with the proper amount of tortilla chips.

Archie dumped the tacos in the middle of one of the beds and set the chips and guacamole on the small night-stand between them. Splinter promptly took a chip, and I opened the drawer in the table so he could snuggle down for his dinner. We dug in, and I groaned with contentment at the amazing flavor of the tacos. But I quickly noticed Bentham's expression.

"What?" I stuffed a wayward piece of beef back into the corner of my mouth.

"You like these?"

"Um, yes, because they're freakin' delicious."

Her face coiled up even more, and she set her partially-eaten food down in front of her. "If you say so. I think they're disgusting."

We erupted, shouting at her about being picky and a Guild elitist. If she was going to join our little rag-tag posse, she needed to learn to slum it a little. She finally relented, scooped her taco back up, and continued to eat.

"I'll get used to it," she mumbled.

"That's a good thing since we're running low on money," Ally informed us.

Archie had finished eating and was inventorying our supplies. Dog went to the door, and Archie let him out. I knew he was going to guard. He was weeks away from the full moon when he would change into his human form. I liked that form. I wondered if I'd be alive to see it again.

I shook the doubts from my head and looked at Splinter. He sat in the drawer and glared at Bentham. Every time she glanced at him, he did his best to look menacing and even managed something similar to a growl. Eventually, the agent gave up on her taco and tossed it down, then brushed off her hands.

"Breaking into The Heights won't be easy."

I agreed. "We need a plan. And supplies."

We brainstormed for a few minutes and came up with a list. When we finished, Archie looked it over.

"I'll do what I can," he offered. "I might be able to call in some favors. But I don't know of any way to get into The Heights apart from the keys, so it will be a challenge."

"Breaking in is only part of the problem," Bentham added.

"What do you mean?" I asked.

Bentham listed the issues. "We know Rand or The Council, likely both, are compromised, which means that Hobbes could be in The Heights or at least someone who knows where he is. But it's not a small place. We aren't talking about a building here—this is an entire realm. So, we get there and figure out how to break in. Then what? We need to know where to look."

"We can try to find a Hobbes follower on Earth and question them," Ally suggested.

"We've been trying that for months," I pointed out. "No one knows anything about Hobbes. His followers get their orders and intel either from drops or from people who get it from others in turn. It's like the game of Telephone of the Damned. No one can trace it back to the source."

"I might have an idea," Bentham offered. "It's risky, but it might get us what we need."

"What is it?" Archie asked.

"There was a criminal the Guild never caught, a dangerous Farsider who the Guild suspected of being in cahoots with Hobbes. Of course, we never got a straight answer about that. We knew where they were, but never had time to go after them."

"Why not?" I asked.

Her eyes moved over to me. "Because all our energy was always focused on you."

I lunged at her, but Ally caught me by the back of my shirt and yanked me back.

"Enough," she ordered. "You have to settle this. I know there's been some bad blood, but we're all on the same side now. We can't have you two breaking out into fights all the time."

"Fine," I muttered. "This criminal. Can we go after them? Maybe they'll have the intel we need."

"As I said, it would be risky. This person is a dangerous target. There's no way of knowing how they'll react to us or if we could get anything out of them."

"That makes it all the more likely they'll have the info we need. As for getting it out of them, leave that to us."

CHAPTER NINE

One thing I learned during this road trip was that cars are far easier to operate when you have the keys. Ally was fantastic at hotwiring, but it got tiresome having to try to act casual and not look suspicious every time we had to start or stop the Oldsmobile. It's not like we weren't already fairly conspicuous. It was a burgundy Oldsmobile.

Regardless of the complications, one day and a lot of dog fur in my face from sharing the backseat later, we got to where Bentham directed us. Which, by the looks of it, everyone had forgotten was there. Approximately located in Middle of the Ass of Nowhere, Midwest, the town obviously hadn't been lived in on a routine basis in many years.

A piddly roadblock was in place across the main street, but it had long since been broken and tossed aside. These old buildings didn't have residents or businesses anymore, but I was sure they were a hoodlum's paradise.

Only, we didn't see any of those, either. It was simply eerie, quiet streets, overgrown yards and planters, and dark windows.

"This reminds me of Centralia," I observed as we stepped out of the car and onto the broken street.

"What's that?" Archie asked.

"It's a town that was abandoned decades ago. It was a happy little place where everything was normal. Then people complained about steam coming up through cracks in the ground and a strange smell. Then a boy fell into a sinkhole and almost died. They figured out that the coal mine under the town had caught fire and was burning throughout the entire area. There was no way to put it out.

"They had to relocate everybody who lived in town, then abandon it. The only real difference is they leveled the buildings there so they wouldn't catch fire if the flames made it out of the shaft," I related.

Ally looked around, an expression on her face that said she was lost somewhere in her thoughts. Finally, she wagged a finger toward one of the buildings.

"I know this place. Not well since I've never been here or anything, but I think I've heard of it."

"Why would you have heard of it?" Bentham wondered.

"Ally is a journalist of the unexplained." I waved my hand dramatically.

"I write for an online magazine researching urban legends, hauntings, and the paranormal...all those things that people don't understand. Where people go missing, dead people show up with no apparent cause, things that shouldn't exist are sighted, or whiffs of a conspiracy come to light, I'll be there," Ally explained.

"Why would that bring you here?" Archie asked. "It doesn't look like there's been anybody here since they packed up and left."

"There's no graffiti," I commented. "The roadblock was broken, but it doesn't look like any of the usual shady stuff has gone down."

"That's because people are terrified to come here. This is a place I meant to investigate at some point but never got to. It wasn't high on the priority list because there wasn't any evidence."

"Evidence of what?" Archie asked.

"The monster," Ally told him.

"Well, shit." I turned to Bentham.

"Don't look at me," she protested. "I knew the location. You said you could handle what was inside."

"The rumor," Ally continued, "was that people tried to come here and take it over. Make it a squatters' camp. Or at least a good place to do urban spelunking. But a few people came and never went home. They simply disappeared. Then another group went, and one person came back. They were so scared that they wouldn't talk about what happened but said there was something awful here.

"That was it. After that, people stopped coming. It's a great story, but there's no concrete evidence. No one would give the names of the missing, and there are no pictures or anything to confirm that there's a monster. So, it got pushed to the bottom of my list."

"Seems you were destined to be here," I told her. I drew in a breath. "All right, Bentham. Let's do this thing."

Archie handed me two boxes, then offered me the shield I thought was destroyed when we encountered the Vrya.

"It's fixed now," he told me. "Should work fine. Put the boxes in your pockets and don't open them until you need a weapon. The magic is powerful but temporary. Keeping them open might make them unstable."

"Thank you." I fastened the shield around my wrist.

Archie offered Bentham a magical knife, but she shook her head.

"What's wrong with it?" Archie asked.

"Runes are an abomination," she answered. "Magic wasn't meant to be mixed with baser elements from The Near."

I rolled my eyes at her. "Let me tell you something. That car that brought us here was most certainly derived from The Near. You sought my help, and I'm only a lowly Near-sider. So I suggest you get over your little bias and use what you have available to you."

She shook her head again, and Archie pulled the weapon back.

"Fine. I'll use what materials I saved and keep working," he said.

"Good. Ally, Dog, I need you two to hang back," I instructed.

Ally grabbed my arm and pulled me a few feet away. "What are you talking about? You want us to let you wander off into the sunset with a Guild agent? Haven't we risked our hides for months now trying to prevent exactly that?"

"Yes, but that's why I need you to stay. I still don't trust her. No matter what she says, there's something weird about this. I need to keep two eyes on her. And I'll need you and Dog to save me if things go wrong. If you're in there with me, you could be in as much danger. This way, there's a chance of getting me out."

Ally finally nodded. "All right. But don't wait. Don't try to tough anything out until the last minute. If something is off or you think you're in danger, call for us."

"I will." I walked back to Bentham while tucking the boxes away. "You ready?"

She nodded, and we walked farther into the deserted town. I hung back slightly, letting her get a couple of steps in front of me. She noticed and glared back.

"What are you doing?"

"If something happens, it's happening to you first."

"Thanks for the camaraderie."

"Are you dead?" I shot back.

"Not at the moment."

"Then I'm super friendly." I glanced around at the dark buildings and remnants of the lives that used to be there. "So, I'll take a wild stab in the dark and say those trauma-tized trespassers told the truth when they said there was some kind of monster in this town."

"Yes," she answered flatly.

"Fantastic. And the people who didn't come back after their little exploring missions? Probably not the frame of the governmental structure leading the resurgence of society here, huh?"

"Not likely."

"Ground up and turned into half-brunch, half-runes?"

"Far more likely."

"Perfect. What are we working with here? Vampire? Troll? Cyclops?"

"Drakaina."

"A who?"

"You don't know the drakaina?"

"She hasn't made it onto my Christmas card list, no."

"Do humans have a name for half-human, half-dragon hybrids?" Bentham wondered.

"Excuse me?"

"You have names for all kinds of hybrids. The sphynx, siykoy, sirin. What do you call half-human, half-dragon hybrids?"

"Creepy as all hell and wholly unnecessary," I retorted.

"Well, that's essentially what this thing is. His name is Batista. He is one of a rare species with both human and dragon attributes. This one likes to lean toward dragon. They don't show up on Earth very often because they're far too conspicuous. Most live in The Heights. But this one isn't welcome there anymore. The intel the Guild has says he's been hiding out here since he became a fugitive," she explained.

"So, claws, spines, a tail, the whole dragon thing?"

"Yes. I guess you've never encountered one?"

"No. But, if I'm going into this thing with you, I might as well keep the 'new things I never thought I'd do' theme rolling," I added.

"Good. You see that warehouse up ahead?"

"It's a little difficult to miss."

"We should look there," Bentham advised.

"All right. Let's check it out."

We approached the warehouse cautiously, but there was no sign of movement. I tried to take note of all the windows and doors as we walked around the building's perimeter, everywhere that wasn't completely boarded up and might be an easy hatch for a Harbinger or Guild agent attack.

"There." Bentham pointed to a door.

"Wait. We don't know what's in there yet. We need to stay calm and take our time." Bentham grunted and ran for the door. A blast of magic shot from her hand as she thrust it up toward the sky. "Damn it. So much for fucking stealthy."

A half-dragon. I knew Ally told me something about dragons in my pop culture catchup lessons, but hell if I could remember what it was. As I bolted through the door and into the warehouse, the only thing that came to mind was a steel seat. Or a golden chair. Something like that. I made a mental note to ask her what it was, assuming I survived.

CHAPTER TEN

The magic blasts stopped, and there was an eerie silence. Bentham had run deep into the building, but Splinter and I had hung back, barely venturing beyond the entrance while my eyes adjusted and I got a lay of the land. It was dank inside and smelled vaguely metallic.

Boxes with what looked like hastily packed papers and items an office would typically have were everywhere. An open container near the door held a tangled mess of wires and computer mouses. Mice? Mices? I never knew what the plural of a computer mouse was.

I stepped forward as my eyes slowly acclimated to the dim light in the building. I could tell it was massive. The walls had cut-outs like for tiny cubicles, and didn't reach even a tenth of the way to the ceiling. It looked like an old warehouse that had been temporarily converted to one of those cold-calling scams.

A broken headset and a loose paper covered with at least a year's worth of dirt and grime had "WARRANT" across the top in bold red letters. A grey footprint of a boot in the center told me that whatever they had been up to here had ended with handcuffs. A fire-blackened file cabinet sat on an equally singed section of the floor. Nothing else around it had any trace of damage, which told me something that had a unique control of fire had been here.

Bentham had said 'dragon,' but I couldn't quite believe her. No matter how much experience I had with creatures of The Far, I couldn't comprehend that a real-life dragon could be a thing. In the distance, I heard laughter and a sound like leather whipping around. It was unmistakable.

It was a wing. I could imagine two of them lifting a great beast with horns and scales above the ground as it spewed white-hot death on us. Splinter ran up my arm and settled on my shoulder, then hid in my hair.

I slowly made my way across the room by hugging one wall so at least I couldn't get blasted from behind. I tried to squint and see what was above me. Shadows danced, but I couldn't discern whether it was because something was up there, or a trick of the faded, grey light coming in from high windows. I gripped my switchblade out of familiarity. Even if I were going to use another weapon primarily, this was my go-to. My trusty failsafe. My fingers tightened around the handle, and my thumb lightly brushed the button.

"You are ill-prepared, human," came a rumbling voice from somewhere in the darkness. It reverberated off the walls and felt like it surrounded me and vibrated through me. "What is a human with Near weapons to a creature like me?"

"Slick, stay out of this," Bentham shouted from some-where farther away. "I know how to deal with him."

"Slick?" the booming voice asked. "Ahh, the exalted one. The one who caused The Problems."

"Ahh, the mysterious dark dragon-thingy. The one who is annoying the fuck out of me," I shouted.

"You dare to challenge Batista?" it boomed.

"Slick, shut up. You're giving away your position," Bentham shouted.

"And you aren't?" I called back.

"Enough. Both of you come to me so that I can drink your blood," the voice of Batista the man-dragon called, closer now than it was before.

Splinter's tiny nails dug into my neck as he hid deeper in my hair. He would fight when the time came, but until things went sideways, he preferred the warmth and safety of one of the most annoying places he could be. Thank-fully, I was used to it. I reached up to stroke his fur to calm him, and his nails retracted a little.

A shuffle from the other side of a cubicle drew my attention. I pulled out the switchblade, ready to attack, and quickly rounded the corner. I had to stifle a shout and slide down onto my ass when Bentham rounded the corner ahead of me, and we suddenly came face-to-face. She crouched so we were close as we threw our backs to the cubicle wall.

"What are you doing?" she whisper-yelled at me.

"Coming to find you. What were you doing?"

"Coming to find you!"

"Well, ya found me. Now, what are we going to do about this thing?"

"Before I had to blow my cover, I was sneaking up on it from behind. Now he knows I was trying to do that, so I have to figure something else out."

"Why don't we get him to come to us?" I made sure to keep my volume low. Something told me he could hear everything we said.

"Because he's a fucking dragon, Slick. In a one-on-one, he'll always have the upper hand. If you can surprise him, then you can get him off-guard, maybe injure one of his wings or his throat and keep him from either flying away or fire-breathing you to death." She stopped and looked at the floor for a minute. "Maybe if you go where I was, he might not expect one of us to go back to the same pl—"

I abruptly stood and drew a deep breath. "All RIGHT, ASH BREATH, COME OUT AND FIGHT!"

"What the hell was that?" Bentham whisper-shouted at me when she dragged me back down by the arm.

"Don't worry. He won't come. He wants the upper hand, right? I only want him to give away his position."

"He's right there." Bentham's voice was flat.

"What?"

I spun to see two almost human-looking legs at face level. One reared back and soccer-kicked me in the jaw, which sent me sprawling backward. I landed hard on a spinning office chair and took a circular ride while it careened backward. When I finally faced the right way again, I saw magical blasts firing into the air and the shadow of the creature dodging them. Suddenly, a stream of orange flame burst forth and illuminated him.

It was more-or-less man-shaped, only three times the size of a normal man and its skin was scaly and ashen grey.

Two horns came from the top of its skull and bent backward, although I could see where a hat could easily cover them.

Thin, leathery wings beat slowly but powerfully to keep him aloft, but I got the impression that it took some effort to get airborne. The scales wound in patterns of black and red along his sides. His eyes burned a bright yellow.

"Slick," Bentham called from somewhere among the cubicles, "remember our plan!"

"We don't have a plan," I called back as I shuffled to my feet and went behind where the flames seemed to come from.

"He didn't know that, dammit," Bentham yelled back exhaustedly.

"Oh, right," I muttered and rolled past a now-melted cubicle wall.

The man-dragon hovered in the center of the area, deep in a labyrinth of cubicles. Getting to him on the ground would require solving the Mid-Management Nightmare Puzzle of a room, or, perhaps, doing something a little dangerous. While the danger had its appeal, I decided to pocket that for a just-in-case. For now, I would try to find my way through.

Splinter hopped out of my hair and took off ahead of me like he knew what I was thinking. He rounded one corner and disappeared from view. By the time I got to it, he had barreled back and headed in the other direction.

I followed him deeper into the cubicle labyrinth. I was passing a mostly intact desk when it exploded in a ball of flame. When I looked up, I saw the man-dragon's legs above me.

"Aw, hell no." I jumped off a desk, grabbed the Farsider's leg with one arm, and hoisted myself up in one motion.

He cried out in surprise and sent flames down on the floor where I had been, but I was already wrapped around his waist and yanking my switchblade from my back pocket. I flipped the blade out, ready to gut the son of a bitch, when a wing wrapped around me and cloaked me in total darkness. Then a sharp talon on the bottom caught the back of my pants and yanked me hard.

I soared through the air and felt heat burn the soles of my feet as he shot flames after me. He was impossibly strong, and my first plan had gone to hell in a handbasket. I tucked to protect myself as I crash-landed in a graveyard of half-empty filing boxes. I took a moment to recover and realized I wasn't seriously hurt. Somehow, I'd landed safely enough that I'd only have a few bruises that would be super sore tomorrow. I stood, ready to give it another round when I noticed that not only did I not know where I was in the room anymore, but worse, I'd lost my switchblade.

CHAPTER ELEVEN

Fire rained down on another part of the room, and a white arrow shot into it. There was a momentary pause in the flame, then it came down again, harder and more intense. Parts of the large warehouse were now aflame, and it looked pretty grim for the idea of getting out of here unsinged. Bentham was somewhere among the cubicles, using her magic to try and knock this thing down, and I was now lost in the maze with no switchblade, and freaking sore.

Splinter, who must have dived off me as I careened to the floor, galloped up to me, sniffed my face, and tried to get my attention. I rolled to my right and tried to put my weight on my knees and hands. Everything hurt. I was *so* going to kill this fucking dragon.

"Slick, any time now," Bentham shouted from much closer than I expected her to be.

"Yeah, I'll get right on that. Thanks," I yelled back. When the words finished echoing around the room, a ball of orange flame exploded a few feet from where I stood, and I took off in the opposite direction.

The warehouse ceiling was still pretty dark, and I could only see where the dragon was when it attacked. It didn't leave a lot of options for capturing or even hurting the damn thing. I rummaged in my pocket for a rune I had stored for a situation similar to this. It was for the stupid Fae creatures, but a dragon was close enough. I got my hand around the grip and pulled it out.

It was a marvel of design and a great example of how Archie's work was getting much better. At least insofar as weaponry went. His gadgets still left a little room for improvement. This one looked like a tiny box, nearly weightless, but I knew what was inside. I pressed the button and placed it on the floor—no sense in not taking precautions when it came to Archie's designs.

There was a popping sound, and the box unfolded to twice, then four times the size as before. Each time it expanded, it clicked into place, and when it finished, I snatched it up. Bow in a Box, he called it. A second box contained twenty ultra-lightweight Gorgon-tooth rune-embedded arrows. I clicked the button for that as well and set it down to let it open as the sound of wings beat nearby. When the arrows had straightened, I snatched them up and stuck them in a long pocket designed for this purpose inside my jacket.

I needed higher ground to get a good shot, so I ran along the back wall looking for a way up. A set of stacked tables presented an opportunity. I hopped on them and climbed until I reached the third set, then looked around.

Still not high enough, but there was an office not far from me that had a ceiling.

Above it was a ladder built into the wall that led to the roof. When I scanned the warehouse ceiling, I saw that beams ran across from one end to the other, and one was only a few feet from the top of the ladder.

I calculated the distance, sprinted at the wall, then hit it at an angle and ran sideways as long as momentum would carry me before I jumped off and somersaulted onto the office ceiling. As I landed and it sank a little, I realized I hadn't accounted for whether it would hold my weight. Still, it didn't completely give way, and I gingerly stepped back to the ladder. I climbed until I could reach out and touch the beam, then grabbed hold after pulling the bow around my shoulder. I hung upside down for a moment, then worked my way onto the metal and carefully walked to a crossbeam, where I knelt to get a lay of the land.

Batista circled no more than ten feet below me, and I saw Bentham scurrying as she charged up a magical blast. Blue electric energy bubbled up in her hands, and she shot it forward in a ball that grazed Batista's tail and fizzled out a few feet past him. She was quickly running out of energy and would need to rest for a little while to build it back up, so I needed to do something.

"Slick, whenever you're done taking a nap, I could use some help," she yelled from her spot, then ran.

Batista turned and loosed a stream of flames that engulfed the area where she had been and caught the wall on fire. It wouldn't be long before they engulfed the entire building and we would all die in here. I pulled an arrow from my jacket and set it in the bow.

I could barely feel it sliding into position since it was so light. The magic in the rune made it almost weightless to the user but would take the weight that should be felt and multiply it on impact. I pulled the bowstring and arrow back and aimed at the man-dragon's neck, figuring it was as good a place as any. I tracked it for a few moments, then let fly. It soared through the air silently but missed.

It continued, then exploded into a desk and sent it into the air in pieces. Batista took a hard right in the air and made for the remnants. It would only be seconds before he figured out where it came from and came after me. The leathery wings beat strongly as he hovered over the spot, and I drew another arrow. I had a mere moment to fire before he figured it out. He turned toward me as I nocked and aimed. His eyes met mine on the beam above him. I exhaled.

As I released, he flew backward, blasted in the chest by a magic shot from Bentham. The arrow soared and crashed into the wall behind him. It knocked some of the bricks out of place and allowed sunlight in. Unfortunately, it also created a backdraft as flames shot through the side of the building with a sudden whoosh that sucked out most of the air in the room.

I felt dizzy and lightheaded and had trouble catching my breath. Everything spun, and I was aware I was so high up a fall would likely injure me or maybe even kill me. I had to stay focused. I had to keep it together.

I tried to shake it off by clenching my eyes shut as my hand grabbed the beam for support. I drew a deep, heaving breath and for a second, everything settled. I opened my eyes.

The man-dragon barreled at me at full speed. He was only feet away, and I didn't have time to avoid him. He would hit me. I had two choices. One was to try to absorb the impact, hold on for dear life, and hope I could get somewhere to land that didn't kill me and wouldn't be on fire. The other...

I grabbed an arrow and pushed its sharp end up at the last second. Then I clenched my legs and let my body sag backward so that I hung halfway off the beam. Batista swung low over me, and the arrow dragged a line of blood from his chest down into his leg. He cried out in pain and crashed into the far wall. As he did, he shrank some, and his leg lost some of its scaly veneer and became more flesh-like.

"He's hurt," Bentham shouted from below. I wrenched myself upright so I could see her. She stood, somewhat recovered, and flicked her eyes from me to the man-dragon now crawling from the wreckage of the former office equipment he slid into. "We have to work together, or else he'll kill us."

"I have an idea." I stood and quickly made my way to the ladder. "I'll get him in the open. Be ready."

I expected an argument, but none came. Instead, she was gone when I got to the floor, apparently finding a place to fire from. I had one last plan, and it had to work. I snapped the bracelet's two moon-phase activators together and ran into the center of the cubicles, now decimated and on fire.

"Come on, motherfucker, let's dance!"

A roar filled the air. I turned to see Batista rising high above me. Blood dripped from his body, and the area around his wound had become human-like skin. His face contorted in a sort of half-transformation between man and beast, and he roared again. Then he turned and aimed at me like an archer before he exhaled a blaze of fire and tore through the air toward me. I activated the bracelet's shield.

The flames bounced off it, but the scorching heat raised the temperature of the metal wrapped around my wrist and burned me. I screamed, matching his roar as I held tight and waited for Bentham to make her move. He was nearly on me now, only a few dozen yards away. I didn't know how much longer I could hold on. I clenched my eyes shut.

"Now!" I shouted.

A bright yellow blast of magic filled my vision despite my closed eyes and blew me backward. Batista crashed to the floor mere feet from me. Electric yellow ropes tied him down and wrapped around his face to block his mouth. I watched, fascinated, as his face contorted still more and became nearly human—bald, bloody, and beaten. He struggled against Bentham's aethermancy magic with unbelievable power. But none of his rage or his strength mattered.

We had caught ourselves a dragon.

CHAPTER TWELVE

"So, are we going to drag this thing out of the burning building or what?" I asked as Bentham made her way beside me.

"He'll shrink. His kind always does when they're hurt. He'll be a little large, but more like a normal male human in a few moments. You can see his leg is already turning," She pointed.

"Yeah, I noticed that when I stuck him with the arrow," I proudly agreed.

"Too bad you couldn't hit him with one normally," she grumbled.

"I'm sorry, I've never had to shoot a half-dragon man-beast thing out of the air with a fucking bow and arrow before." I faced her.

"Don't get hot at me, Slick. I'm only saying if we had gotten him earlier, either one of us, we wouldn't be in a fast-burning building that will soon attract a lot of attention."

"Whatever." I waved it away. "Look, he's already shrunk some. Let's try moving him."

The magic Bentham used was strong, but not very taxing. She pulled on what I thought of as magic ropes for lack of a better term, and I grabbed his talon-feet and tried heaving him with us.

After we shuffled and dragged his struggling form to the door, I kicked it open and drew a deep breath. It was as if I had never breathed fresh air before, and my lungs ached for it. Still, we had no time to waste and kept pulling Batista until we had him fully outside.

"Where is your friend?" Bentham referred to either Archie or Ally.

"They're bound to see the smoke since I'm sure they aren't too far away."

Almost on cue, a van I hadn't seen earlier screeched around a corner and stopped at the front of the building. The sliding door crashed open. Dog jumped out and growled at Batista's prone body, and Archie appeared in the sunshine.

"Come on, we have sirens incoming!" he yelled as he hopped out.

The three of us muscled Batista's restrained form into the vehicle, then I stopped and patted my pockets as I looked at Bentham, a dawning horror washing over me.

"My switchblade is still in there," I mumbled and turned to go back in. Before I got a step, Bentham's hands latched onto my shoulders, spun me around, and tossed me into the van.

Ally punched it and got us onto the highway and to the outskirts of town in record time. While she drove,

Bentham silently tied Batista to one of the captain's chairs with Far vine-laced rope and slowly lessened the magical hold she had on him. When Ally pulled off the road at an old, decrepit, abandoned fast-food building, I slid open the door for some fresh air, and he blinked in the light.

"I'll let you talk," Bentham grumbled in a low whisper close to Batista's face, "but I swear, if you don't tell me what I want to hear, you're in for far more pain than you're already in, you hear me?"

For a moment, he sat there unblinking as his yellow eyes burned holes in Bentham. She stared right back, unfazed. Not for the first time, she impressed me. He nodded curtly.

"Good." She waved her hand in front of his face.

"A Philosopher." He nearly spat the word out of his mouth. Then his head swiveled to look at me, penetrating through me with his demonic eyes. "And Sara Slick."

Bentham jammed a fist into the side of his face, and he howled in pain. When his head rose again, fresh blood trickled from his nose, and he smiled through it.

"How the world is changing. The New Order is upon us."

"The New Order? Is that what you call it?" Bentham demanded.

"What I call it. What it is. The scale had tipped, and now it is being leveled. Balance is coming."

"I don't care about your balance. I don't care about your Order. I want to know the details." Bentham straightened.

"You help her?" he motioned at me with his head. "If you work with this one, you're a traitor to your kind."

Her hand flew so fast I barely saw it. It buzzed with

electricity as she backhanded his jaw, and this time, he rocked backward with a searing burn across his cheek. His face turned my way, and he stared at me as he drew a few deep breaths and spun back to her while roaring.

He curled his lips and tried to breathe flame, but only smoke came out. His eyes widened, and he tried again. More smoke poured from his nose and mouth, but nothing else.

Bentham grinned. "Special Ivy, grown in The Deep. It's quite good at balancing the scales."

I expected her to back away and continue the interrogation, but instead, her fists flew again. She pounded Batista's body as he writhed. I watched in shock as she laid into him before I finally moved forward, put my hand on her shoulder, and pulled her away.

She glared at me, then pushed her hair back from her face. I leaned closer to the man-dragon and noticed the spit and blood now pouring from his mouth and onto his chest. The wound from my arrow also still gaped unhealed. Despite this, he looked defiant.

"Ok, I guess this makes me the good cop," I said levelly. "First time for everything. Tell us what we want to know, and I won't let her empty your guts on the floor and paint pretty little flowers with your blood."

"Kill me. That's what you'll do. It doesn't matter because Hobbes will kill me now, too. Batista is no more." He laughed mirthlessly.

"You know Hobbes? Personally?"

"Oh, yes. We've met many times."

"Help me stop him. It's the only way you get out of this alive."

His eyes swiveled back to mine, and he took a long second as he thought about what to say. "In The Heights, I use the Lighthouse."

"What?" I was confused.

"That's not enough." Bentham slammed another punch into his chest. He bent over as much as he could and coughed blood onto my clothes. I grabbed Bentham by the shoulders and pushed her back.

"You. Me. Outside, now." I pointed. She turned in a huff and went out the open door. I turned to Archie. "Make sure he doesn't go anywhere and put something on his leg. He's going to bleed out before we learn what we need." With that, I stepped outside.

Bentham stood a few feet away, her arms crossed and her head down like she was contemplating something.

"What the fuck is wrong with you?" I demanded, but she put her hand up with one finger out as if to shush me. I grabbed her fingers and shoved them down. "Oh, hell no, I will not be treated like some annoying child. You lost your mind in there."

"All his kind knows is violence." Her voice was low enough that I had to strain to hear her over the sound of blood pumping in my ears. "If you show mercy, even the slightest amount of hesitation, he'll use it to defy you. You have to destroy his will. Show him he isn't the alpha. Then he'll obey. He can only obey or destroy."

"He was bleeding to death! I think he knew he wasn't King Shit anymore," I yelled, but the sound was cut off by something behind me.

"Aw, dammit," Archie yelled from inside the van.

"Great, now what?" I turned to head back inside. Before

I could, Archie exited the van, but he wasn't alone. Inexplicably, Batista was loose and had the Ivy wrapped around Archie's throat, pulling him like a leash as he got out of the van.

"One move and he dies," he grumbled. His scales were returning on his legs, and his face was morphing. He seemed bigger than before. "Batista will live and die by his power!"

"He's regenerating," Bentham said under her breath. "In a few seconds, he'll be able to breathe fire again."

I squared off with him, my mind racing for something I could do to stop him. I was blank, completely plan-less. He yanked on the Ivy and Archie moaned in pain. I stepped toward them. Batista snapped around to me, but as he opened his mouth to speak, Splinter appeared on his shoulder.

"I said one mo—ah!" he cried.

Splinter bit him hard on the neck. Smoke billowed from Batista's mouth, and his grip on the Ivy loosened. I dove at Archie, grabbed the Ivy and pulled it away, then wrapped my arms around him and rolled with him to safety. Batista reached up to grab Splinter, but he was already running down the man-dragon's back to his leg. He tore at the wound, and it opened again, blood gushing out. His job done, Splinter took off for the van.

A *whum* sound crushed into my skull and made my eyes water. I looked back at Bentham, who had both arms outstretched with fingers splayed. I looked at Batista, who now rose in the air, but his wings were stationary. Bentham was doing it to him, whatever it was. A purple glow covered his body, and his mouth was open in a silent scream.

"Where can we find Hobbes?" she yelled at the stricken creature.

"You will die by Hobbes' hand, as will all traitors to the cause," he yelled back. Bentham's jaw set and her hands moved apart. Batista broke open in the center, starting at the top of his skull. His brains spilled out like a runny egg, and suddenly, his entire body ripped in half.

Blood rained down on us, and I turned my head to block it from getting in my eyes. When it finally settled, I looked up. Bentham stood above me with the sun behind her in a cloudless sky, her face in shadow with barely discernible features. Blood splattered on one side of her cheek and above her eye.

"We have to go. We have to break into The Heights."

CHAPTER THIRTEEN

This is bullshit.

That was the only thought running through my mind as I stood in the center of an open courtyard and waited for someone to try to kill me. Somehow, in the afterglow of sudden respect at seeing Bentham tear a dragon dude in half, I agreed to a plan that involved me being bait. At least Splinter was with me, hiding in my jacket and giving me an extra sense of security in case things went sideways.

When things went sideways, that is.

The darkness outside the small number of overhead lights in the courtyard cast deep shadows all around me. I had to trust that Bentham and Archie and Dog were all in place because I was super exposed. They would be the first ones able to get to me, while Ally kept an eye out for an escape route should we need it. A sound like a kicked rock caught my attention, and I looked toward the place where it came from.

"Archie?" I asked in a voice that was supposed to simulate fear, but if I was honest with myself, it was more real than feigned.

"If it isn't Sara Slick," a familiar voice said from the darkness. A step into the light revealed Thrash's sinister flat nose and beady eyes. He was smiling, and someone came up beside him. "Let me introduce my new partner, Mill. Mill, meet Sara Slick. Kindly go and take her down."

Mill, a mountain of a man with shoulders as broad as a bus, barreled toward me with uncanny speed. I ducked away and rolled. His hands glowed a bright red, and I looked into the shadows near me. Any second now...

White light filled the horizon. Bentham charged, her arms out in front of her as she blasted into the center of Mill's chest. Thrash took a step back in surprise. I grinned as I stood.

"Everybody, now," he commanded, and a host of other Philosophers came to his side. Now it was his turn to grin as he looked between Bentham and me.

"Bentham, you son of a bitch. Working with Sara Slick? How fucking predictable."

"Save it, Thrash. We don't need to fight. You need to listen," she ordered.

"The only thing I'll listen to is you begging for your useless, traitorous life," he spat. Suddenly, his wall of Philosophers charged, and the fight was on. Bentham shot blasts of magic into the oncoming horde. I spun and kicked into the crowd and connected with multiple chests, jaws, and legs.

I ducked a fist and grabbed the waistband of one of them, and pulled him toward me as a blast of Bentham's magic hit him directly in the face. His features melted into a vortex of skin and blood, and I dropped him. Bentham reached into her jacket and tossed something at me, which I caught in mid-air, unable to believe what I saw.

"Where did you find this?" I snapped the switchblade open and turned to slice an oncoming Philosopher as he missed a blast and a grab, and caught only the pointy end of my blade in his chest.

"You dropped it when Batista flung you. It landed right beside me." She sent out another blast that took out one of the last standing Philosophers.

"Thanks." I jammed it down into the injured bad guy and made sure he wouldn't cause more trouble, ever again.

"Don't mention it." She turned back to Thrash.

Dog charged into the fray and took the arm of one Philosopher about to ram his glowing fist into the back of my head with him. He disappeared into the melee, but I heard him thrashing and growling as well as the surprised and horrified shouts of Philosophers who were unprepared for a monstrous, vicious dog to be in the battle with them.

Other familiar sounds made their way to my ears as I dodged what looked like a massive spear that crackled with energy and it buried itself into the body of a charging Philosopher behind me. Archie's unhinged and delighted laughter bubbled up as a rune he made activated and tore into a crowd of Philosophers standing in a group near Bentham.

Soon, the battle died down almost all at once. Around us, the littered bodies of a dozen Philosophers lay in various states of burned, beheaded, stabbed or knocked out. Bentham faced Thrash head-on. "Come on, Thrash.

You knew they were only cannon fodder for me. Either you fight me yourself, or you give up now. One way or the other, you're coming with me, and you know it."

"I'd rather die," he grunted.

"I can arrange that." I popped up behind him. His focus had been on Bentham, so he hadn't noticed me go around. Now he was stuck between us. He had a choice to make, and I had a feeling I knew which one it would be.

Like I figured, he raised his hand to hit me with a magic blast, but I quickly lifted a leg and smashed him in the head with a hard kick. He stumbled to one side, and I ran after him, jumped, and landed a knee to his lower back. He crumpled to the ground, and I seized his arm, then twisted it and bent it backward. After locking him in an armbar, I wrenched back until I knew it was close to snapping. All it would take was a little twist.

"Give it up, Thrash. She doesn't want to hurt you, but I sure as shit do," I yelled.

"Human scum," he managed to blurt out through my legs muffling his face. I jammed one against his mouth again, and he tried to turn away from it as he clawed at them with his free hand. I saw his fingers glow as he tried to work up his magic. Just one little twist...

What the hell. I owed him one.

His shoulder snapped as I pulled back, and he howled in pain. Suddenly, he went very still. I yanked on the arm and spun so I was now behind him and pressing him down into the ground with his broken arm pulled up behind him. He was quiet now, refusing to cry out in pain, but I knew I had him. Whatever will he had to fight was temporarily gone. Bentham slowly walked up to us and crouched in front of him.

"Thrash, things aren't what they seem. You have to listen to me," she insisted. "Sara isn't the enemy. Hobbes is. We can keep this war from getting any worse, but you need to work with me."

Thrash stayed quiet, and I wrenched his arm up higher. He struggled against me but didn't make a sound. Bentham crouched lower so she could see his eyes.

"Thrash, you could help us. We could save everyone," she pleaded. "Wasn't that what we always hoped we would do as Philosophers? Be called upon to be heroes? Now is your chance. Take it!"

Thrash wasn't listening. It was obvious she wasn't getting through to him, and as much as I wanted to think she could change his mind, that she could save him, I knew it wouldn't happen. We needed to cut our losses and go, then figure out another way to get into The Heights.

I felt Splinter shift around in my pocket and a second later, he scrambled down my leg. He could be a courageous little thing when he needed to be, but I didn't know what he was doing and worry filled me. Maybe this wasn't courage. Perhaps he'd panicked and ran for it. In the overall fight or flight response, he very well could have tipped over the edge and decided to go for flight.

Suddenly, Thrash glowed a dull orange and roared so loud I winced. The sound was demonic, and I realized it was because of the intense pain he was going through. He was growing, using his magic to outsize us so he could escape, but with his broken arm, it was excruciating.

He reached an incredible size that towered over both of

us before he took off and shrank as he ran. Bentham went after him, but I caught her and pulled her back. Dog took up a defensive position between us and Thrash's disappearing figure and growled.

"I have the key."

"You what? How is that possible?" she sputtered.

A tiny hand poked out of my pocket, and I pointed at it. A smug-looking Splinter had returned to my pocket a moment before and now sat with the key in his mouth.

"Him. Don't underestimate Splinter. He might eat way too much junk food and be terrified of a large proportion of situations he encounters, but he can steal with the best of them."

Archie rushed up to us with several robes in his arms. They were clearly homemade. The sewing on them was wonky, to say the least, and one appeared to be made out of several different scraps of fabric haphazardly put together like he'd taken the leftovers from when he made the other robes and crafted the last one from it. They weren't perfect, but that was fine. They would work in a pinch, and we were most certainly in one.

"Go," he urged. "You don't have much time."

I nodded and shrugged into one of the robes. After drawing in a deep breath, I let it out and turned to my crew. They couldn't go on with me, and I knew it. We'd call too much attention to ourselves if we all wandered through The Heights together. This had to be only Bentham and me. Besides, there was still work to do here, and they needed to do it.

"Archie, thank you for the robe and all the runes. Even the ones that nearly killed me."

"I'll keep working on them. And I'll practice talking to humans," he promised.

"I'll hold you to that. When all this is over, I'm bringing you out to a bar, and I want to hear a whole conversation."

He extended his hand, and we shook. He squeezed it, then let me pull him in for a fast embrace. I turned to Ally and felt tears sting my eyes. That wasn't acceptable—there was no crying in inter-realm warfare. We stared at each other for a few seconds. No one would ever be able to understand everything she and I went through together or the depth of our friendship.

In so many ways, she was the only link I still had to the person I used to be. When I looked at her, it reminded me that there was more to me than the person who was beaten down and brutalized by The Deep. She still held the old me in her mind and heart, and that was invaluable. One day, maybe I would get to know that person again.

We suddenly jumped toward each other and hugged tightly.

"Thank you so much," I whispered into her hair. "I couldn't have gotten here without you."

"Don't you dare disappear for another ten years," she replied tearily. "I'm young enough to handle your crazy now, but I'm not doing it in my thirties when I'm supposed to have my shit together."

"Duly noted. Love you."

"Love you."

I pulled away from her and crouched next to Dog. I ran my hand over his head and had the sudden compulsion to tell him I would miss him most of all. It unexpectedly tugged at my heart and made the tears sting more. I wished he could speak to me. I wanted to know he understood how much he meant to me and how much I appreciated him. I could always count on Dog to protect me and look out for me. I wanted to tell him all of that and to thank him for all that he'd done.

"Be good," I told him instead.

I knew he would understand.

"We have to go," Bentham urged. The portal glowed white but seemed too small. It was as if the fabric of reality itself had cracked, almost like a tear in a dress. It warmed and cooled, and its color shifted along with its size. I was mesmerized by it but had to tear myself away. Bentham made a complicated motion with the key, and it hummed a tune almost out of my range of hearing on the low end.

I looked at my friends again, tried not to let myself imagine it could be the final one, and turned away. The portal was now wide open, large enough for both of us to walk side by side. I braced myself for whatever might be on the other side. With a deep breath, Bentham and I ran through the portal and into The Heights.

CHAPTER FOURTEEN

I had never felt more out of place in my life than when Bentham and I snuck through The Heights. That included the first night I got tossed into the tiny cell in The Deep. That was disturbing and insulting, but this place was intimidating. I never gave myself a lot of time to think about the antithesis of The Deep.

I was far too embedded in the prison's filth and horror to let my mind wander to what its opposite would be, and what it would be like to experience the place the Philosophers considered so pure and perfect. It seemed kind of a futile effort when figuring out how to survive to the next second or kill whatever was trying to keep me from that goal took up most of the space in my mind.

But now, I was experiencing it. When I looked around at the exquisite surroundings, I felt like nothing short of a contaminant. Not that I was all that bad. My hygiene had significantly improved since leaving the rundown motel outside of Charleston that I'd loved so dearly, and I'd gotten into the habit of looking almost like a normal person daily. But The Heights was far beyond the parameters of anything I'd ever seen or thought of.

Everything was bright to the point of glowing and so shiny I wouldn't have been surprised to see groups of tiny people running around polishing every surface continuously. A glance above me showed three suns overhead and a scattering of sparkles across the sky around them like they were shedding glitter.

And here I was, wearing a HomeEc project robe and sneaking around with someone I still wasn't completely convinced wouldn't turn on me in some massive trap, with a rodent of an unknown kind in my pocket. And Dog fur on my clothes.

There wasn't even the luxury of Bentham and me being the only ones wandering around. If the streets were empty, at least I wouldn't feel like I stood out so much. But as it was, the whole place teemed with people. Seriously important-looking people.

Their robes were lush and comfortable but also lined with gold and ruby. The jewels sparkled in the triplicate sunlight, and jeweled crowns bound their hair around them. They walked with an air of superiority and intelligence and dominance over the world around them. I wished I could have the level of confidence just once in my life that these creatures had every second of their pampered and busy existences.

It was mostly Philosophers, but other Farsiders were mixed in as well, and even they looked well-dressed and stately. I was used to only seeing Farsiders looking like mutant extras from an eighties karate movie, but these looked so much more like aliens. It was silly to think that, but it was true. My only experience with well-dressed, un-thuglike creatures was movies about aliens from before I went to The Deep.

The highly privileged space we were in meant everyone around me looked wealthy and sophisticated. And arrogant as hell. These weren't people I could imagine knocking back a beer with and playing a round of darts.

I did my best to blend in and look like I was supposed to be there. That was the key to all this. It had been the same when I first got out of The Deep and integrated myself back into the human world. Bentham already fit in. This was her turf, and she already knew what she was doing. I was the one traipsing along without a clue. Not letting on was what I needed to do. Act like Bentham. Walk like her. Talk like her. Move like her.

Bend it like Bentham.

If I could dissolve into the crowd around me and not call attention to myself, Bentham and I could make it through The Heights and to the Lighthouse without inci-dent. That was the goal. All I needed to do was make everybody around me think I was one of them, and not let on I was a person they all feared and considered a bloody mass murderer.

It probably would have worked out better if I hadn't told myself that while also staring at the suns and the sparkles around them. The bright blue hue of the cloudless sky contrasted the golden-yellow orbs even more. I squinted as I stared up at it and wondered what kind of birds would dare to ruin the perfect vision of The Heights' horizon.

The strange sky fascinated me so much that I didn't pay

attention to where I was going and bumped into someone in front of me. The impact bounced me back a few steps, and Bentham reached out to grab me and keep me on my feet.

I rebounded and saw the man I ran into turn to look at me. He bowed deeply. The gesture caused several long tentacles that seemed to be attached somewhere on his head to slide out from his hood and dangle in front of him.

"I am sorry, fellow Being, for disrupting your path. I apologize for interrupting the flow of your existence, and it is my sincere hope it will promptly restore itself. Forgive me."

Stunned into momentary silence, I sincerely hoped he would continue on his way. Instead, he straightened and looked at me, obviously expecting a response. There had to be a specific way I needed to reply, but I didn't know what that was.

Time kept ticking, and Bentham stood a few feet away, staring at me with widened eyes. This would have been a fantastic time for me to develop telepathy spontaneously, but no such luck. I was on my own with this one. I flung myself into a deep bow and let my arms swing out to the sides.

"Oh, Great Tentacled One, I have received your sympathetic vibrations. Bumping into you was a great joy to me as it perhaps will allow some of your fabulousness to rub off and grant me hope and buoyancy as I continue to flow through my existence. I accept your apology and raise you a blessing upon your existence. Live long and prosper."

I brought one hand around in front of me, then separated my fingers into the V-shape with my thumb pulled out to the side. It was all I had, but when I straightened, it was apparent that wasn't the response the Farsider expected. He stared at me in surprise, and his tentacles seemed to recoil the longer he did. Bentham suddenly stepped between us.

"She knows you meant no harm and did not see you as an interruption. You are but a part of her existence now, and she appreciates the contribution you have made. She can only hope she has done some good for you and that the moments you have spent here with her are to keep you from a danger that may have befallen you along the way."

They bowed to each other, the situation apparently resolved, and the Farsider continued. We were about to move when another man stepped up in front of us. He scrutinized Bentham, and his eyes narrowed.

"Bentham? What business do you have here?"

She didn't reply but gave the man a fearsome glare. He buckled under her menacing look and backed away, then moved down the street at a quicker pace than he'd approached.

"Come on," she ordered, and we continued on our way.

"What the hell was all that about?"

"The Heights is a pure and privileged place," Bentham reminded me. "Propriety is paramount here. Harming someone or interfering with their life as they are living it is considered a great offense. So, you apologize. It's an expected ritual that goes a little further than the usual 'I'm sorry,'" she explained.

"That's kind of an understatement. I had no idea what to say. I felt like Archie."

"You sounded like Archie. That could have gone quite badly, fast."

"I thought people here didn't like to bring harm to each other," I pointed out.

"Not if it isn't considered appropriate," she countered matter-of-factly.

"Lovely."

"We need to be careful. If you keep bringing attention to yourself like that, we'll never make it."

Sticking close to Bentham throughout the rest of our walk through The Heights kept me from getting into any more sticky situations. I noticed several more people looking at her, obviously surprised to see her there. She had a key. I knew she belonged here. But it was clear she wasn't here often, and this wasn't an expected appearance. Yet, no one stopped her. She was known, and no one wanted to be the one to mess with the great Bentham.

We finally reached a massive building, and Bentham gestured at it.

"You can't be serious." I looked at her, then back at the gaudy, gold-encrusted building. "That thing is the Lighthouse?"

It was huge and elaborate and covered in decorative scrollwork and dramatic touches. It looked more like a temple of some kind than a tool.

"Yes. Now, come on. The suns will soon set."

CHAPTER FIFTEEN

The Lighthouse stood on the edge of a rocky shore, and there were two paths to access it. One was a cobblestone road that led to a wide area that I assumed was for parking whatever celestial vehicles they drove here. The other was a winding path that turned into an alley and wound around the side of the building. One large streetlamp stood near the Lighthouse, and one at the end of the road, but none between.

My Spidey-senses told me that was good because as the light of day slipped away, and the suns hid behind the Lighthouse from our perspective, we could move down the path with the cover of shadows to help conceal us a little.

The suns had gone beyond the horizon by the time we reached the top of the building, leaving a cavalcade of starlight in the black, inky night. When I thought of a lighthouse, the first thing that came to mind was the tall, looming beacon that swept back and forth and lit up even the darkest of nights across the ocean. It was kind of the point of a lighthouse—something big, bright, and a little obnoxious to keep sailors from smashing into things.

That was the same thing I envisioned for this lighthouse. I thought Bentham would pull a lever or light a big fuse and a giant light would burst out over The Heights. It would be glorious. Only, that's not what happened. Instead, Bentham took out a small candle and waved her hand over it. The wick lit, and she settled the candle into place.

"That's it? I mean, props on the whole creating fire on the wick thing. That was cool. But that's what we're using as our beacon? I thought it would be something with a lot more pizazz."

"Pizazz draws attention. It doesn't matter how big the light is, only that it's visible. And that will be seen by those looking for it. Now, we need to wait."

We went inside and found a place to sit. I hated waiting. I hated it more than almost anything. Especially when the reason for it wasn't assured to work. This wild, half-baked idea was the best we had, but there was nothing we could do except sit around, twiddle our thumbs, and hope it worked.

If it didn't, there was no way to find Hobbes. I tried not to let myself stew on that thought as we sat in silence. There was nothing to say. All that remained was time and tension.

I tried to focus on the best-case scenario, almost willing it into being. I hoped that whoever showed up in response to the Lighthouse lighting up was Hobbes. It was that simple and that unbearably complicated. Not for the first time, I tried to imagine what he would be like. He framed my family for terrible crimes condemning me to The Deep. He sent his goons to destroy the world I loved.

I tried to envision him, to put myself in the position of finally facing off against him and how that would feel. Part of me could only imagine him to be some sort of monstrous, overwhelming creature, or an imposing, dead-eyed man who would look fearsome from the moment he walked into the room. But the terrifying part was I knew that didn't have to be true.

If there was any lesson I took away from my time in The Deep and the mission I'd been on since escaping, it was that evil doesn't have a specific look.

"So, all those sparkles around the suns. Was there another one that blew up at some point, or are those three simply really fancy?" I asked a few minutes later when the silence started to get to me.

"As far as I know, there wasn't a fourth sun at any point." Bentham sighed.

I nodded. "Just fancy. Got it."

We fell back into silence again for a few moments before Bentham turned to me.

"What is that creature you carry around?"

"Splinter?" I patted my pocket to make sure he was still okay. He popped his little head out, and I scratched the top of it before he nuzzled back down. "I have no idea. It doesn't really matter. He's my buddy. We found each other while I was in The Deep. Well, he found me. He scrambled into my cell one day. I don't know what was happening to him, but whatever it was, he wasn't happy about it. After a while, we became friends.

"He's gotten me through some of the hardest times in

my life. After Solon died, I was so alone. The old man was the one thing that kept me from completely falling apart in there. He taught me what I needed to know and kept me strong. Then, he was gone. I had what he taught me and my switchblade, but that was it. Then Splinter came along, and I had someone again."

"It's incredible you survived in there," she confessed.

My eyes cut over to her.

"I know. Far better than you do. That's the thing. The Guild thinks they know The Deep. You think because you've seen it or you control it that you understand what goes on in there and what the prisoners go through. You have no idea. Now, don't get me wrong. There are some truly ridiculously gross evil creatures in there, and they deserve whatever they have coming to them. But there are others…"

My mind went to Berne and the horrible death he suffered for no other reason than his mind had slipped away from him. I let out a breath. "Let's just say that you people have the market cornered on cruel and unusual punishment."

"Sometimes it's warranted," Bentham pointed out.

"And sometimes it's only a seriously messed up custom. Which I've noticed is a trend. Let's talk about this place."

"What do you mean?"

"This," I flailed my hands around over my head to indicate the area around us. "Is The Heights."

"Yes."

"The pure and exalted place set aside for only a few," I continued.

"Yes."

"Why?" I prompted.

"Why?"

"Yeah. Why? Why is this place so special it has to be thought about in awe and talked about in hushed tones?"

"Because, as you said, it's a pure realm. It's set aside as a reminder of the way things used to be," she explained. "Before The Near and The Far became one."

"And why aren't most Farsiders allowed in here?"

"To maintain its purity and protect its value," she claimed, clearly getting bristly about my questions.

"But why would you do that? If this place is supposed to be some sort of nostalgic throwback to when The Far was a separate glorious place and the Farsiders were able to roam around in peace without having to deal with the drudges of the Nearfolk, why keep them out now? Isn't your job to help them?"

"There are rules, Sara," Bentham started.

"You aren't above me anymore," I pointed out. "In my opinion, you never were. But you're not going to talk to me like I'm a child or your pet. If you're going to run with us, you'll call me Slick."

She drew herself up, inhaled, and held it for a few seconds like she was hoping the air would calm her down. She let it out.

"There are rules, Slick. Rules are essential to ensuring the smooth operation of any society. Yes, it is my job to help Farlings, but that doesn't mean there aren't divisions in society. There is a hierarchy, as there is in any other culture."

"Not among humans. Not like this," I insisted.

"Of course, there is. You can't honestly tell me you think

all humans are equal. That they all have the same opportu-
nities and get treated the same way," she snapped.

"Maybe not, but it's not like this. You've tossed aside the
majority of your people. They're abandoned to scrape and
scramble and figure shit out for themselves. They're locked
out of The Heights, The Deep is a horror show, and the *Pax*
forces them to remain underground on Earth, so they're
isolated and alone. No wonder so many of them turn to
crime."

I was going to continue, but she reached out and
grabbed my arm. Her head snapped to the side as she
strained to listen.

"Quiet," she ordered. "Someone is coming."

CHAPTER SIXTEEN

A robe-draped figure appeared in the distance. As they stepped forward, I could tell it was a woman, but little else. Whoever it was seemed confident, though, walking with purpose until they stopped a few feet away from where we hid in the shadows.

"Come out, come out, wherever you are," sang the voice of the robed figure. It sounded so familiar, but my brain would not place it. It couldn't be. The person that was coming was supposed to be Hobbes, but that voice...I knew that voice. That was...

"Rand?" Bentham whispered, half to herself. "What the hell is she doing here?"

"I don't know, but she obviously has the answers we need." I reached for the lightsaber-like weapon that I had snatched from Archie before we went through the portal.

"No," Bentham whispered and put her hand on my shoulder to push me back down. I shrugged her off but stayed sitting on my heels. "Rand is, well, she's extremely powerful. Fighting her is a losing battle, trust me. Not without a lot of planning. She's cunning and has incredible control over her magical powers. We don't want to fuck with her unless we have a plan."

"I have a plan. I'm going to whip her ass."

I stood before Bentham could stop me, and the back of my head crossed through the light to cast a shadow at Rand's feet. She turned to me, a smirk on her face as she pulled the robe's hood off her head.

"Sara Slick. I knew you'd come. It's about time I ended you once and for all."

"Got that backward, *padre*. It's about time someone beat some sense into you," I retorted and ran for her.

I pressed the button on the side of the blade, and it dropped into place. Electricity buzzed off it. I raised it into a fighting position when Rand's hands went into the air but skidded to a halt as the roof broke underneath me.

It shook, and I fell on my back, hard. Parts of the concrete snapped in half and shot up, nearly swallowing me whole. I struggled to my feet, now only a few yards away from Rand, and leveled my sword again.

She barely moved. Only an almost imperceptible nod of her head, but it was enough that I caught it. I looked in the direction she nodded and saw more shadows—lots of them. They came from seemingly nowhere and stayed slightly beyond the light so all I could see were their glowing eyes. There were trolls and giants and cyclopes, and Philosophers and Farsiders of all types stepping up at her call. I swiveled my head to the other side of her and saw many more approaching to stand in place.

And Bentham was nowhere to be found. She had warned me against taking this fight, and she was right. Not only was Rand powerful, but she had a damned army with her too. I readied my sword and tried to think of an escape plan. Bentham had no doubt hoofed it back to the portal and left me to die.

If I could make it back there, at least the battle would be on my turf, and Dog and Ally and Archie could chime in too. I took a small step back and felt a strong wind blow me back into place. Rand was gently waving a finger in the air as she controlled a nature element and forced me to stay.

So much for escape.

"Surrender now, and I will cast you into the pit of The Deep. I cannot promise I won't kill you later, but I will at least spare your life today."

I let the words echo around me. Die today or die tomorrow. That was the option she gave me.

"Or," I countered, "you could surrender now, and I can save your army of dummies here from a lot of pain and embarrassment."

The faintest hint of a smile stretched across Rand's face. "Death it is."

They charged.

A blast of white fire scorched a line of charging Farsiders before they could reach me. I looked up to see Bentham leap into action with her hands sizzling with magical power. She landed beside me and nodded. Together, we turned to the charging Farsiders and went to work.

I slashed with the sword, cutting through arms and legs and stabbing into torsos almost indiscriminately. The world was red with rage and desperation and the smell of war. Magic singed the air with octarine fire and lit up the night so bright that it was near as light as day. Rand stood a few yards away and watched as Bentham and I cut our way through her forces.

Our backs stayed to each other, fending off troll after troll, hellhound after hellhound, Philosophers and freaks alike. My eyes kept flicking to Rand, who focused on something as she stared into her curled hands. Something was going to happen, and if Bentham and I were going to survive a few minutes longer, we needed to do something about it.

"I have an idea." Bentham grunted. "You take Rand. I'll hold the rest of them off."

I opened my mouth to object but had no words. Rand was an all-powerful magician of The Far, and I was a human with an electric sword and a switchblade. And years of rage.

Bentham suddenly leapt into the air and crashed down onto the roof while leading with her fist. A shockwave of energy circled out from her and cleared the area of bodies, both living and dead. Except us. And Rand. She stood against it as if it was a low tide in summer. A circle surrounded us now, crackling with purple energy. Rand and I stood in the center. She smiled. I smiled back.

It was "go" time.

We both ran at each other and met in the middle. I slashed with my sword, but she dodged it, then expertly kicked my hand and made me drop it. I drove my shoulder into her stomach, and she doubled over and fell back a step. As I moved closer, she brought both hands up in an axe-handle that caught me on the jaw and straightened me up with the impact. I was momentarily dazed, and she used the opportunity to charge up a magical blast. I ducked at the last second, and the attack flew over my head. It singed my hair and landed in a second wave of charging Farsiders, and nearly melted them on the spot.

I kicked and smashed her knee with the heel of my boot. She crumpled to the concrete, but spun on her hip and got back to a standing position. She swung a fist, but I hooked her arm and rammed a few punches into her ribs.

Her free hand grabbed the back of my hair and yanked me down. Then she jumped to drive her knee into my face. I rolled away at the last second, then kipped up and soccer-kicked her in the face as hard as I could.

It drew blood.

I had hurt Rand the powerful, and for a moment, everything seemed to pause. She wiped her face with her hand, saw the trickle of red, then stood. I tried to ready myself for whatever magical blast was coming, but she surprised me by attacking with her fist. A right cross caught me hard, and I heard the bones around my eye socket crunch under it. I went down hard, and she leveled a kick to my ribs that left me unable to catch a breath. I rolled away from her, trying to create some distance, and watched as the blood that trickled down her face slowly stopped. Her swollen nose, which I was sure I had broken, evened itself out. She regenerated almost immediately.

I scrambled to my feet, but she shot out thin waves of yellow energy, ropes of pure magic, that wrapped around my feet and pulled me down. It was the same aethermancy power Bentham had, and Rand used it to stop me and drag me to her.

As I struggled against the magical rope, she reached down and clasped my feet with her hand. I watched in horror as it enlarged until her fingers closed around my legs. It was a power I had only seen Thrash use once before, and she wielded it now as her entire body grew to three times her size.

She lifted me with ease and smashed me onto the roof like I was a blunt instrument. She could have used me to play baseball. Instead, she whaled me into the concrete three times, then released me. The magical ropes let go as I sprawled on the hard surface. Blood poured from my eyebrow, my nose, and my mouth. I was in tremendous pain, but I wasn't out yet.

"Now, for you," Rand announced, and I heard her turn toward Bentham.

"Hey," I mumbled as I got to my feet, then spat out blood and what I was reasonably sure was a tooth. Rand stopped cold and turned to me.

"I'm not done beating your ass yet."

CHAPTER SEVENTEEN

She hadn't fully turned before I was on her and whaling away with wild fists. There was no method, no discipline, no measurement in those strikes. They came from deep within me, spawned by many years of rage while in The Deep, the sorrow of losing my family and friends, and my anger at the life taken from me without my permission. I hit her with all the pent-up emotions inside me and felt her bones crunch under my fists. If I went down, I wouldn't do it like a punk.

Rand tried to shake me off, but I hung on tenaciously, ripping and clawing her when I couldn't swing. Her fists clenched to make magical blasts, but I was too close.

We tumbled to the rough surface beneath our feet, and I gained the upper hand as I straddled her and laid in with my elbows to her face as hard as my body would allow. Everything hurt, but I didn't care. I was going to die today, and I was going to do it while punching this woman as hard as I could.

She bucked underneath me and rolled me over until I was under her, then raised one hand to build a magical blast. I clawed her face, hoping that if I went now, it would be with one of her eyes in my fingers. But before she could blast me, a beam of energy hit her on the shoulder and knocked her off me. I looked over to see Bentham, one hand shaking as it tried to hold the barrier, but the other outstretched toward us. She had saved me from certain death.

I rolled toward her, slower now as the adrenaline wore off. Rand was hurt and regenerating. If we were going to get out of here with any chance to survive, it probably had to be now. I had barely moved within reaching distance of Bentham when she blasted another shot at Rand.

"We should go."

I nodded. I didn't have much else left.

"I'll hold them off while you run for the portal," Bentham directed.

"Hell no," I responded. "We both leave, or we both stay."

"You'll be killed. It doesn't make sense. You can end this. Let me help you."

"You can help me by staying alive," I retorted.

A roar filled the air behind me, and I turned. It was too late. Rand was back, her power regenerated and her body growing, only this time with slightly less size. Perhaps she wasn't wholly restored after all. I pulled my switchblade out of my pocket and snapped it open.

"I can't hold them much longer." The light of Bentham's magic waned.

"You won't have to." I stood and charged Rand, using

everything I had left. I held my switchblade up, poised to throw it and dive onto her, and hoped I could get a few stabs somewhere that she wouldn't be able to regenerate fast enough. I was one step from leaping when her left hand swooped in front of her.

I froze.

My toes were still on the roof, but the rest of me was airborne. Yet, I was frozen to the spot. I could move my eyes but nothing else. Everything was numb and immobile. I screamed through a closed mouth as I watched her snicker and blast Bentham. It knocked her down hard, and the energy field that protected us from the rest of Rand's army disappeared.

Rand looked at me again and waved her arm in the other direction. I fell a few feet from where I stood when the momentum returned, but my brain didn't catch up to it. The switchblade dropped a foot away, and I scrambled for it. My fingers touched the grip.

A boot smashed into the back of my head and sent me face-first into the concrete. Everything went black for a moment, then blurry. Shadows danced above me, with watery images of Rand standing above. One of my eyes was swollen shut. The other was trying to make out details like I was standing at the bottom of a pool looking up. Blood filled my mouth, and I coughed it out. Feet away from me, Bentham stirred, hurt, burned, and spent.

I had nothing left. I was finished.

I was going to die.

Forget that.

The pain radiating through my body took my breath

away, but I didn't stop trying to drag myself back up to my feet. Rand wouldn't take me down like this. She might have gotten the upper hand, but I wouldn't give up. I wouldn't give her the satisfaction of watching me lie in the dust and die. As I struggled, she arrogantly swaggered up to me.

"Here we are," she gloated. "After all this time, I'm finally facing the infamous Sara Slick. You know, I envisioned this moment many times, but never quite like this. I guess that goes to show reality can be so much better than fantasy, can't it?"

"It took you and an entire fucking army to try to bring me in," I said through gritted teeth.

Rand laughed. It was cold and merciless and made my blood boil.

"What did Hobbes promise you?" I demanded. "You betrayed your oath. Doesn't that mean anything to you?"

"Oath?" she mocked. "To what and whom? No sworn promise is worth what I know waits for me."

"Hobbes won't share power with you. You know that. Hobbes will destroy you like everyone else when you're no longer needed," I spat. "And all of this will be blood on your hands."

"Hobbes won't have to share power. Don't you see? Haven't you figured it out yet, Sara Slick?"

My stomach sank, and my heart jolted up into my throat.

"You?" I seethed.

"That's right. You've been hunting down the boogeyman, and all along, Hobbes has been right here in front of you. It's me. I'm the boogeyman. I'm Hobbes."

I struggled to move but couldn't. Everything in me wanted to jump up and rip her to shreds. My mind ran in a million different directions, and I felt like screaming.

"I would say it's nice to meet you again, but that isn't true." The words were flippant and dismissive. She smiled and licked her bottom lip. "After all, I've known you your whole life."

"What do you mean?"

"Maybe you should have a little heart-to-heart with your mom." Rand simpered, then tilted her head to the side and sneered. "Oh. I guess you can't do that, can you? Maybe soon, though. She can tell you all about it when you join her in hell."

The fury rushing through my veins fueled me enough to pull me up to my feet again.

"Talk about my mother again," I grunted as I forced my knees to respond and hold my weight, "and I promise you, it will be the last thing you ever say."

I faced off against Rand, ready to give my last breath to fight her if I had to. It seemed she had the same thought.

"You can't imagine what your pathetic world is about to go through." She paced back and forth for a few seconds, then stopped sharply directly in front of me. "Too bad you'll be dead before you can see it."

I felt in my pocket and found a final rune, one of the old ones Archie designed for me what felt like a lifetime ago. I wrapped my fingers tightly around it and pulled it from my pocket.

"Maybe. But I'm taking you with me as a souvenir."

I activated the rune and threw it. The Lighthouse

exploded and collapsed around us in flame and debris. Rand screamed. I stood in place, wanting to watch her get broken into pieces. Instead, I felt Bentham grab me by the wrist. I looked at her and had only a second to see the flash of the key before she opened the portal back to Earth and yanked me through it to escape.

CHAPTER EIGHTEEN

The blood on my face wasn't drying fast enough to keep up with the new blood coming from my injuries, and I was sure if someone snapped a picture of me right then, I would look a hot fucking mess. I didn't give a shit.

What remained of me was alive and back on Earth, but we'd failed. We didn't do what we set out to do and were right back where we started. Literally. The motel Bentham smuggled us into using a combination of magic and memory erasure that I was positive wasn't in the Guild handbook was only a few miles away from my family's house.

After everything we'd gone through, she sucked me through a portal minutes away from where I first got yanked into The Deep. There was probably an epic poem or a folk song or something in there somewhere, but I didn't feel particularly creative.

A knock at the door stopped my pacing, and I glanced through the peephole. I expected it, but I wasn't going to throw the door open without looking in case the Harbingers had followed us.

Ally stood on the other side of the door, shifting her weight back and forth anxiously and glancing around like she was waiting for the same thing. The bag clutched to her chest bulged, and the symbol emblazoned across the one in her other hand was even more proof I was close to home. It was also proof my mind was too tangled up. I didn't even care about a bag of tacos from my favorite place.

She grabbed me in a tight hug as soon as the door opened. I stumbled back a few feet and dragged her into the room with me as I kicked the door closed behind her.

"I'm sorry it took so long for me to get here," she apologized.

"You managed to shave about three hours off the usual drive time for that trip," I pointed out. "You did fine."

I had called her the moment we entered the motel. She was surprised to hear from me so soon. This wasn't the plan. And she certainly wasn't expecting me to be back in Charleston already. But she got on the road and came to me as fast as she could.

I expected nothing less of my best friend, but somehow that made me even more upset. I let out an angry sound that was somewhere between a growl and a yell and resisted the urge to kick the air conditioner. I needed to vent my tension and anger, but now wasn't the time to alert our motel neighbors and have the human cops swarm us. There would be time for that nonsense later.

Ally crossed the room and set the tacos on the small round table against the wall, and the other bag on one of the beds. Opening that one revealed a collection of medical supplies along with tubes and vials containing various powders and liquids. Unless CVS had gotten into the shady magic-based healing game, those had to come from Archie.

"That was our chance," I told her. "Our one chance to get into The Heights and end this shit and we blew it."

Ally picked up some of the supplies and gestured for me to come over to her.

"Let me fix you up. Archie sent some of his concoctions. I'm not sure what they do, but hopefully, it will help."

"Why does it matter?" I flopped down on the bed.

"Because you have to leave this room eventually, and if you look like someone put you through a meat grinder, the humans will notice," she pointed out.

I tried a smile through the searing pain of her pressing a cloth soaked in something purple against a deep cut across one cheekbone.

"Aww. I like how you say 'humans.' You're acknowledging everybody."

"Yeah, well, not all the non-human folk are bad. Don't want to lump the Farsiders all together and make it us against them." She picked up another vial and shook some powder over the purple goo. "Consider me an anti-speciesist."

"Me, too." I swatted her hand and leaned away from another dose of the powder. "What are you doing? Adding sprinkles?"

"This stuff is supposed to get you as close to normal as possible. You didn't exactly get out of that situation unscathed."

"Trust me, I'm aware. That whole plan went to hell. We were supposed to get into The Heights, find Hobbes, smash him into tiny pieces, and save the world. I mean, in a way, I guess that part did work out for us. We found Hobbes. It turns out she's fucking Rand."

"I can't believe it."

Bentham's voice surprised me. She hadn't said a word since we got to the motel, and I'd almost forgotten she was there. She sat curled up on the other bed and stared into the distance. The entire situation had shaken her, and she hadn't wrapped her mind around it yet. She shook her head, then turned it to look at me.

"Are you all right?" I asked.

Ally leaned in for another swipe at my face, and I pushed her away. She tried again with the same result. A sneak move toward my chest that ended up at my forehead finally succeeded in getting more of the goo and powder on me, but I got up from the bed before she could do more.

"I didn't know," Bentham stated, her voice soft and high with emotion. "I didn't know."

I shook my head as I sat on the edge of the bed beside her.

"No one thinks you did. We know you wouldn't have gone through all that to feed me to Rand. If you setting us up in the mobile lab would have been a stupid plan, that... THAT would have been…. Wow."

I hoped Bentham would at least crack a smile, but she didn't. She kept staring at me, looking at me like she was seeing me for the first time.

"I've been working for a terrorist my whole life." It

sounded like her throat was squeezing tighter and tighter as she spoke. "Rand is the most powerful Philosopher I've ever known. And she's responsible for all this. All this time, we thought we were fighting against this cruel subversive leader, and we were doing her bidding instead."

"You didn't know," I reiterated. "You had no idea what was going on. That's not your fault."

"I should have known. Something should have told me what was happening."

"Like you said, she's the most powerful Philosopher there is. Someone that powerful won't make it easy for you to figure out what she's doing," Ally reassured her. "That was part of her plan. You can't let yourself think that way."

"How else am I supposed to think? I helped her. Everything that's happening right now is partially my fault," Bentham insisted.

"No, it's not," I said forcefully. "You didn't know, and you wouldn't have done it if you did. You stepped up. You risked your ass to defy Rand as soon as you thought something strange was going on."

Bentham's eyes met mine intensely. "You are completely innocent. All this time, you've been innocent. I'm so sorry."

I reached over, took her hand, and squeezed it. "Thank you."

"What now?" Bentham asked. "What do we do next? We can't simply say this is over."

"No," I agreed while shaking my head. "This isn't over. Whatever Rand has against me, she won't stop until I'm dead."

I got up and paced the room. Ally and Bentham watched me as I walked.

"I don't get it. Why make it personal? She has every advantage, and her plan is almost complete. Why spend so much effort going after me?"

"Because you keep stopping her plans." Ally shrugged.

"That, and she clearly hates you." Bentham smiled. "And after spending some time with you, I can understand the instinct."

"No." I ignored the insult. "It's more than my charming personality. And it's more than the work I've done since coming back to Earth. She said she's always had it out for me. I don't know why, but everything points to this being about me, or at least my family. Everything from framing my father to Rand mentioning my mother, screams personal. I need to know more."

"What are you going to do?" Ally asked.

"I need to go back to where it all started," I told her. "I need to go home."

CHAPTER NINETEEN

"I need someone I can trust." The realization of what words I uttered hit me hard. The person I said them to wasn't Ally, my longest dearest friend, or Dog, who had been loyal and vicious in my defense, or even Splinter. It was Bentham. The former Philosopher who had hunted me forever, and had more than once tried to kidnap me and send me back to The Deep.

"I need an army. And I need someone to command it. I need you, and anyone you think you can get on our side," I instructed. "We need more help if we're going to make it out of this."

"I might know some people. It won't exactly be an easy sell."

"Don't try to sell it," I advised. "Tell the truth. Tell them what you know, and if they believe it, great. If not, well, we'll deal with that then."

"I'll do what I can," she assured me.

"The most important thing is for you to stay safe. If you can't find someone who might be able to help us, go somewhere you can hide. Hunker down and keep to yourself, and don't let anyone know where you are."

"I'm not going to sit around and not do anything," she argued. "You might think this is personal, but it's not only about you. Hobbes…Rand is going down, and I'm going to make sure I'm a part of it."

"Then get yourself ready. Find anyone who you think we can trust, load them up with whatever weapons you can get your hands on, and lay low until it's time."

Bentham nodded, gathered a few things into her bag, and left the room. Ally turned to me when she was gone. "Bold move, sending her away. She's pretty powerful."

I shook my head. "We'll need her, but not for what's next."

Ally's face dropped, and some of the color drained from it.

"You're really going home? I don't know how your family will take all this."

"They won't have to. Not yet. Right now, it's about the house. Rand said she's known me my whole life. She mentioned my mom. I don't know how, but my mother is involved in all this. At least, she was."

"But, Slick, your mom…" Ally started cautiously.

I nodded. "Don't worry. It doesn't involve a Farside seance ritual or anything. I didn't mean I need to talk to her. You know how Dad is. He doesn't let anyone know, but he's ridiculously sentimental. He keeps everything. After Mom died, he left everything in place for a long time, but he finally packed up all her things in boxes and tucked them away in that extra room he used for storage on the top floor. If it's all still there, I might be able to find something that could explain the link with Rand. It's worth a try, at least. What are Archie and Dog doing right now?"

"They're off working on a secret project together."

"Oh, dear lord." I sighed. "Well. I guess whatever happens can't possibly turn out any worse than all this already is. Right now, I need to get inside my house."

"Without your family noticing," Ally added.

"That would be ideal."

"Then I guess it's time for me to visit. I haven't seen them for a few months, so it won't seem all that out of the ordinary if I go now."

The punch of emotion that hit me was unexpected. I was glad Ally had kept up with my family and watched over them during the years I was gone. It made me feel better knowing at least they weren't alone and both of them had each other's support. But I couldn't deny the twinge of jealousy and envy that came when I thought about how much she experienced with them that I never got to.

My sisters were so young when I was taken. The time I was gone was longer than the time I was with the younger ones, which meant they were far more familiar with her than they were with me. It made my heart hurt, but also made me more determined than before.

"Give my father a call. Tell him you'll come by in a little while," I urged.

She nodded and took out her phone. As it rang, she looked me up and down.

"Archie knows his stuff," she commented.

She walked out of the room to talk, and I went into the bathroom to look in the mirror. One eye was still a little puffy, and there was some discoloration on my face, but the deep gashes and cuts had reduced to scratches. I used a washcloth to wipe away the blood and was impressed by how much better I looked. Having clothes that weren't torn and bloodied would've helped, but I was thankful for small victories.

When Ally came back into the room, she told me my father was expecting her. I scooped up Splinter, and we left. My nerves increased as we drove toward the house. Everything around me looked both familiar and strange.

I knew where I was, but so much had changed during my time in The Deep, it was like someone else had heard about what I remembered and drew their version of it. It was the same, but not. As we turned onto the street where I grew up, I told Ally to stop.

"Let me out here. You can't pull up in front of the house with me in the front seat."

She nodded and pulled up to the curb. "Okay."

"See how smoothly you did that? Didn't hop up in the middle of a yard or anything," I teased.

She laughed, but I saw harsh emotion in her eyes. This wouldn't be easy for her, either.

I climbed out of the car and snuck through the yards toward the back of the house. The tree still stood, and I hoped muscle memory would kick in. Scrambling up the branches felt like old times, and it wasn't until I got to the window that it occurred to me, I didn't really know what I was sneaking into.

After so many years, my father very well could have changed things around. One of my sisters might have taken over my room. He was sentimental, but even he packed away my mother's stuff after a while.

Looking through the window proved I had nothing to worry about. As I listened to Ally speak unnaturally loudly at the front door to keep my family distracted and me aware of the timing, I carefully eased the window open and slipped inside. Almost eleven years later, he still hadn't fixed that lock. The room looked exactly the way it did the night the Philosophers took me away, right down to the homework assignment on my desk.

Shit. That thing was super late. I definitely wasn't getting full credit for that.

I crossed the room without looking around too much so I wouldn't get caught up in the nostalgia, and carefully opened the door. I heard Ally downstairs, then my father's voice. It made my heart jump into my throat, and I had to fight with everything in me not to run down the stairs to him. But family reunions and intense focus didn't go hand-in-hand.

As I quietly made my way toward the storage room, I heard another voice. It took a second to recognize it, but as soon as I did, the image of a tiny face staring out of the room beside me the night I disappeared came to mind. It was Mia.

The sister I saw walking down the street months ago. The one faint link to my family I'd had since I escaped The Deep. She had grown so much. I wanted to stop and listen to them, but I couldn't. The mission came first.

I made it to the storage room without alerting the household. As I expected, it was still full of boxes and plastic totes stacked there when I was younger. A label on the side of each one chronicled what slices of life were stored inside. It was like a scientist's selection of slides. They could take a sliver of something and put it on glass, slide it under the microscope, and see everything about it. That was these boxes. Someone could remove the items inside and examine them to know about those singular moments in time in each of our lives.

I went to the back corner where I remembered Mom's boxes being and found the stack. When I reached for the first one, I toppled forward and knocked another box off its perch. My body tensed, my mind blanked, and I didn't know what to do.

Downstairs, Ally burst into loud, maniacal laughter. Whether it actually covered up the sound or simply scared the living hell out of my family and they forgot they heard it, no one bounded up the steps to attack the intruder.

I took the box down, grabbed one more, and set them in the middle of the floor. Then I sat in front of them and removed the tops so I could dig through. Rand said she had known me my entire life. She talked about my mom. She might have been merely taunting me.

If she knew enough about my father to frame him for the crimes and create an entire subculture movement with me as the folk villain, then she knew my mother was dead. But it didn't feel like that. I was moments from death, and her confidence had too much cruelty behind it.

The first box was mostly things from when I was young, but when I dug into the second box, I found mementos of my mother's life before she was a wife and mother of five. I sifted through pictures of her and my father when they first married, their wedding, and when they were dating.

She looked so young and beautiful. I still had clear memories of her in my head, but it wasn't a comparison to looking at a picture of her and seeing her wide smile and bright eyes.

As I went back through her life, I carefully scoured each of the pictures and scrutinized them to find anything that might explain Rand.

Then I saw it.

I held a picture of my mother's fifteenth birthday party. I recognized my grandparents' backyard and a few of my distant family members. I even remembered the younger faces of some of my mother's friends, including the very young, very smitten face of my father. A large group of smiling teens clustered around my mother in front of her birthday cake right before she blew out the candles. It looked like a snap from the end of an eighties high school movie, complete with the weirdo outcast off to the side.

I pulled the picture closer so I could examine the odd girl more carefully. She stood several feet away from the rest of the group, looked pissed off and shot daggers from her eyes as she glared out from under a hat. The loner seemed oddly familiar, and it made my stomach sink.

It was Rand.

"What the hell?"

CHAPTER TWENTY

I stared at the picture in my hand for a few seconds while trying to make sense of it. Maybe it wasn't her. Perhaps it was another strange person who had no business in my mother's life and looked like she wanted to destroy all of existence. There had to be plenty of those around. Right?

But no matter how long I looked or tried to justify it, there was no arguing. The angry girl in the awkward hat was most definitely a young Rand. What was she doing at my mother's birthday party?

Splinter crawled out of my pocket and perched on my leg. I put the picture in front of his face and pointed at my mother grinning behind her cake.

"See her? That's my mom. Wasn't she pretty? She was only fifteen in that picture, but she was even prettier when she grew up." I pointed at my father. "And that's my dad. They weren't dating yet, but it wouldn't be long before they were." Then I moved my finger over to Rand. "And you know who that is?" He snarled, and I nodded. "Exactly. Why would she be there?"

Splinter didn't offer a lot of insight.

I highly doubted I would find a drawn-out explanation in scribbles on the back of the picture. That meant I needed more information, and I wouldn't find it by digging through the boxes. Instead, I took out my phone and snapped a picture of the photo, and made sure my hand wasn't visible. It needed to look as much like it wasn't taken in the storage room as possible.

Satisfied with the results, I shot a message to Ally that asked her to show it to my dad and find out if he knew anything. He was at the party and saw the girl, so he had to know something about her. If he could tell me her name or how my mother knew her, it would be helpful.

I stuffed my phone back in my pocket, then cleaned up the pictures and other nostalgic items scattered around me on the carpet. I carefully set the boxes back in place, not wanting to have another incident and call attention to myself. Splinter was poking around the room, and I scooped him up before opening the door to check the situation.

Ally was still talking loudly downstairs when I crept out of the room and made my way back down the hall to my bedroom. I slipped through the door and closed it behind me, then quickly crossed back to the window. Before I climbed out, I hurried over to my closet and grabbed some clothes, then snagged a few things from the dresser and shoved them into my backpack, which slumped on the floor.

Chances were, none of my family ever came in here. If they did and noticed things changed, there was little they could do about it. Hopefully, I'd be able to explain it to them before too long. I tossed on some clothes that fit pretty much the same as they did when I last wore them, and shoved the dirty stuff in the bag as well.

I slung the bag onto my back, then shinnied down the tree and rushed to the corner of the house where I could hover and wait for Ally to leave. I didn't want anyone to see me lingering on the side of the road waiting for a ride. At least here, I was only vaguely suspicious in the yard.

A few moments later, I heard the front door open.

"Thanks for stopping by," Dad said. "It's always good to see you. Don't be a stranger."

"I won't. You, either. You have my number. If you need anything, call me," Ally replied. "Same goes for the girls. Got it, Mia?"

"Got it," Mia agreed.

I wanted to see her. If I leaned around the side of the house enough, I might have been able to glimpse her. But I also might have tangled myself in the garden hose wrapped around its frame a few inches in front of me and ended up flat on my face in the middle of the lawn. Not a risk I could take right now. Instead, I waited for Ally to walk down the porch steps, then ran through the yards again so I'd be ready at the meeting point I'd texted her.

It was too risky to use the same spot where she dropped me off. Neighbors around here noticed things like cars pulling up in front of houses and people hovering around. They'd see if I showed back up and Ally came and got me. Instead, I went the opposite direction and waited in a tree line between two houses I distinctly remembered as giving out awesome Halloween candy when I was a kid.

Shit. I missed Halloween. It wasn't the same, being

surrounded by real ghouls and goblins. And The Deep never had good candy.

She eyed me strangely when she pulled over on the side of the road, and I climbed inside.

"You changed clothes?"

"Yes." I held up the backpack. "Got some extras, too."

"We're on the brink of war, you broke into your father's house to get intel about a monster being in your mother's life from before you were born, and you took the opportunity to rob your damn self?"

I glared at Ally, then pulled my seatbelt around to hook it into place.

"Mom always taught me to wear clean underwear whenever I was going out in case I got hurt in an accident. I can tell you with unwavering certainty there are some accidents in my future."

"Fair enough."

Ally pulled away and did an approximately seventy thousand-point turn to get the car facing the opposite direction, so we didn't have to drive by my house on the way out of the neighborhood. The chance that Dad was still standing at the door or had gone out to get the mail and would see me in the car with her was too high.

"All right. What did you find out about the picture? Did Dad know Rand?" I prompted as we turned the corner.

"Yes, but that's not what he called her. Get this. According to him, her name was Ayn Adams."

"Ayn Adams? She had a normal name?"

"Apparently. She was the weird girl who lived in the house next door when your mom was growing up. Everyone knew her as the creepy neighborhood kid nobody liked. She never wanted anything to do with anyone, and no one wanted anything to do with her. But when your mom's birthday party was coming up, she wanted to be nice. So, she invited Ayn," Ally explained.

"I'm surprised she went," I commented.

"I'm sure a lot of people were. But your dad said everybody assumed Ayn's mother made her go. That whole idea of if you force teenagers together, they'll eventually start making friends with each other."

Splinter crawled out again and climbed up on the dashboard, then leaned over to scratch the button that opened the glove compartment. I pressed it for him, and he jumped inside as soon as the door dropped. A bag of cheese doodles and another of mixed cereals waited for him inside. Ally might act like she didn't like him, but she always made sure to hide snacks for the spiky little guy. He cuddled up to the bag of cereal, and I pried open the doodles so he didn't claw through the plastic.

"That probably worked out swimmingly," I joked.

"It most assuredly did not. Sometime after this picture was taken and while the party was in full swing, some of the boys decided it would be hilarious to bully Ayn. They tried to snatch her hat. Your dad said she always wore one."

"Of course, she did. She was weird and creepy enough with her inherent personality. She didn't need to show off her pointy ears," I reminded her. "I assume they were like that when she was a kid. Philosophers have to grow up from something."

"Well, she was determined to keep that all to herself. She decked the guy who grabbed it, smashed the others' faces in the cake, and stormed out of the party. None of them ever saw her again."

"Really? What happened?"

Ally shrugged. "Your dad didn't know. He kept laughing about that cake."

I stared at her, stunned by the revelation. A thought settled into my mind and tingled on the back of my neck.

"My mother was fifteen when that happened. The same age that I was when they took me to The Deep."

"Holy shit."

Before she could embellish on that, an explosion rocked the ground beneath us and flames shot into the sky ahead of us.

"Fuck," I muttered. "The Harbingers are here."

CHAPTER TWENTY-ONE

A fist crunched into the Harbinger in front of me in time for it to lose any further desire to impale me with its blade-like fingers. That was extremely helpful since I was currently tied up with an eight-armed, foul-smelling jelly beast with a mouth like a vacuum made of saws.

The arm in question belonged to Bentham, who darted around using one hand to fire magical blasts and the other to straight-up wallop bad guys with five fingers of fury. It was impressive, and I would have told her so had I not been struggling to keep my neck out of the slippery octo-asshole that had one arm around my left hand and three others around my waist.

I was about to call for help when a blade whistled over my head and cleaved the many-legged stench-monster's skull. It bubbled and gurgled as it slowly sank to the ground, and a puddle of yellowish pus made my boots sticky.

I turned to see Ally with a grin on her face and a small scratch above one eye. She nodded and faced the group of oncoming Harbingers again, and pulled the sword out of the drizzling goo after I moved out of her way.

"Thanks." I reached in my pocket for my switchblade.

"You know I always have your back, Slick." Ally swung the sword in an arc and slashed a warthog-looking Farsider down his chest. A blast from somewhere in the distance knocked over the next closest two as Bentham continued to create a perimeter around us.

I barely had a chance to join the melee when all hell broke loose. Bentham was first into the fray and blasted the Harbingers with magic and occasional brute force. Ally was next, hacking them with a sword that I suspected was a rune, and had been fine-tuned by Archie to seek out major arteries automatically. Either that or Ally had practiced a lot during her downtime. Maybe both.

"We have trouble," Bentham shouted from several yards away with her head turned toward the crest of a hill.

"I know, there's a lot of them," I shouted back.

"No, bigger than that." Bentham pointed. Beyond her finger, I saw a wall of bodies making their way closer. But these weren't simply Farsiders bent on destruction and pain.

They were Guild Agents.

"Well, shit," I muttered to myself. "This just got a lot more complicated."

The one Thrash had called Mill led the group. He was a mountainous man, but Bentham had caught him by surprise the first time we fought. I knew he'd look for vengeance this time around and certainly wouldn't be as easy to defeat as before.

The day was almost over, and the sunlight waned. It

would soon be dark, which would give us a small advantage. With only the three of us, we'd be harder to find if we spread out, but the daylight exposed us.

A massive but fast cyclops charged me from one side and broke past the fallen bodies of his comrades that Bentham had struck down. She fired a shot at him, but he ducked it, then crouched and leapt in my direction. I rolled to the side to avoid him, but he hit the ground like a rubber ball, effortlessly bounced back to his feet, and reached out to grab me with long, muscled arms.

I aimed a kick at his jaw and temporarily knocked him off his path, then shoulder-blocked him in the stomach and rammed him into the wall of an old abandoned bakery we happened to be near. His body smacked against the brick, and I wasted no time in snapping the switchblade open and slicing through his stomach. He roared in pain as his guts spilled, and I jammed the blade under his chin for a mercy kill.

As I yanked the blade out, I heard a yelp from behind me. I spun and saw Mill firing blast after blast at Ally, who had dived behind a car to avoid them. One of her pants legs was on fire, and she was patting it hard with her hand to put it out. I ran to her while avoiding an orange ball of flame headed my way.

By the time I got to her, Bentham was level with us. She'd been forced backward by the mass of Harbingers and Agents making their way forward. The sky filled with the colors of the Agents' magic and Bentham looked like she was getting tired.

"What are we going to do?" Ally asked as she finally put out the fire. I saw a burn on her leg that couldn't have felt good, but she avoided making anything more than an annoyed face while turning to me.

Before I could answer, I heard footsteps pounding from behind, and I spun to defend us. A shadow dove through the air, rolled when it hit the ground, bounced to its feet, then laid heavy blows on the Harbingers. Its efforts created a space for Bentham to escape and join us behind the car. A creature with a long, detached eye lost its vision when the shadow tore it off him and sent him scurrying away while screaming in pain.

The shadow moved with a vicious precision, and when the last of them was on the ground, dying or dead, the shadow turned. The light of a distant streetlight behind hit it and revealed a long, slender shape, with wild hair and lean muscles visible through a tight shirt. The shadow turned and came for us, and I needed no introduction.

It was Dog. In human form. He wore a glowing red necklace that pulsated with light. My cheeks burned as a smile stretched across my face, and I had to stop myself from running to him. I looked up again. The moon was only a sliver of light in the sky. *That can't be right. It's not even close to when Dog usually turns.*

More footsteps behind us produced the huffing, exhausted, and out-of-breath shape of Archie. He crumpled behind the car with us and held out something in his hand. I took it. The heft of the item meant it was another rune, but I didn't know what it was.

"Archie, what's going on? Dog, how?" I asked.

"It's something I've been working on. A secret project. See that necklace? It's a rune that lets him turn when he needs to," Archie revealed.

"But I thought you hated turning into a human?" I asked Dog.

"If I can help you better in a human form, then it's worth it."

I choked up despite myself. Those words meant a lot to me, and a flicker of a smile crossed his lips. I felt one stretch across mine too. I stepped back and tripped over my feet. Before I could curse, strong, sure hands grabbed me by the waist and pulled me back up.

There was a moment where the two of us were close, too close. Our bodies touched, and I felt the heat of his breath on my neck. I shook my head and stepped back again, this time without tripping.

"Thank you," I managed.

Dog simply nodded.

"Come on out, Slick," a high-pitched and whiny voice called. "It's time to put an end to all this, right now."

I peeked over the car. The only person standing there who could have made that statement was the hulking mass named Mill. That voice? Came out of that guy?

"I mean, I can end it for you just fine, but I have a lot of other shit to do after I crack that faulty voice box of yours," I yelled back.

"Very funny," Mill whined. It was like someone had stuffed a bagpipe into Mike Tyson. Whiny, lispy, and entirely inappropriate for its package.

"I also play birthday parties and bar mitzvahs," I continued while fiddling with the rune weapon Archie handed me. Archie opened his mouth, ostensibly to explain it, but I held out a finger to shush him. "I figured it out."

"Oh, no, but you see," he began, but I was already

standing and brandishing the short wand-looking instrument.

"*Avada Kedavra!*" I shouted and motioned the end of the stick toward Mill. I always wanted to say that. I expected a light, or a magical blast or something to explode from the tip. Instead, there was silence. I looked down at the tip of the wand, then back at Mill, who looked at me expectantly.

"Slick," Archie muttered, "what are you doing?"

"It's a wand." My eyes darted down to him, then to Ally, who smiled the way people do when they want you to know they love you, but you fucked up. I sagged and darted back down behind the car as I dodged a spout of fire from Mill's hand. "Archie, it's a wand. What the hell else am I supposed to do with it?"

"It's not a wand. It's a whip," Archie corrected.

"What?" I was exasperated.

"Watch." Dog opened his hand toward me. I handed it to him, and he quickly stood. I peered over the car as he swirled it high and snapped it forward, then yanked it back.

A low rush of sound filled the air, then exploded near Mill. The ground rumbled like thunder, and the Harbingers and Agents alike stumbled as the earth tossed them around.

"It's a sonic whip." Archie grinned as he watched the road open up in front of us and listened to car horns wail. "It creates a minor earthquake by producing a sonic boom!"

"Come on," Bentham urged, "we have to go while they're distracted."

Without a word, we tore off and headed toward the

alley where Archie had been. Dog and Bentham stayed behind. Bentham fired magic blasts at anyone who got to their feet, and Dog snapped off another sonic boom where the Agents had stood. They doubled back, facing the crowd, and as I neared the corner, I heard Mill's cracking, miserable voice again.

"Your family will get what's coming to them, Slick! They'll all get what's coming to them," he shouted and laughed. A blast from Bentham cut off his amusement when it smashed into his chest and sent him barreling backward. I turned to see him get hit, but Bentham had broken into a full run after firing off the shot.

"Don't worry about him. Let's go," she ordered.

Part of me wanted to go back there and gut him for what he said. To make sure they knew that fucking with my family wasn't on the menu. But Bentham was right— the best way to protect them was to get safe, right now. They outnumbered us, and would soon recover from the sonic whip. I rounded the corner and saw Archie holding the door of the van open as he beckoned us inside.

CHAPTER TWENTY-TWO

I stuffed another of the cold tacos in my mouth as I paced back and forth through the motel room. In the short time I'd spent there, I'd done enough pacing to wear a path in the burgundy carpet. The taco I snatched from the pile dumped out of the bag Ally brought to the hotel when she first arrived was soggy in my mouth, but I didn't care.

The fight had made me angry and hungry, and with everything else going on, a less-than-satisfying taco seemed a decent food metaphor. The rest of the crew had claimed the two beds and the chair near the window.

"It's getting worse," I pointed out. "It was bad enough when the Harbingers were wreaking havoc all over the rest of the world, but now they're in Charleston. This is where they planned to come all along."

"What do you mean?" Dog asked.

"When I was in The Deep, a guy was brought in. Berne. He was fifty shades of batshit crazy, but he seemed to know things about Hobbes that other people didn't know. I didn't have a chance to get a whole lot out of him, but while he ranted and raved, he talked about the coming attacks. He said they would strike at the holy city."

"Charleston," Ally confirmed.

I nodded. "That's when I knew I had to escape. Solon had trained me for years and coached me on how I would eventually get out. It was the only glimmer of hope I had, of course. Him telling me I had what it took to get out and that I would eventually see the light of day again. But I never knew when that would be.

"As soon as I heard Berne mention the attacks on Charleston, I knew I couldn't stay there anymore. It was seriously fucked up that I'd wasted away for ten years for something I didn't do, but I wasn't going to sit around and let Hobbes take out the entire world, starting with my hometown. Fortunately, stealing the key from the Warden brought me pretty close."

"Right to the bar where I was that night," Ally filled in.

I paused and looked at her. She was patching up Archie, who was busily playing with Splinter with the other hand. It was good to see the two of them bonding. She glanced at me and offered a hint of a smile. I could still remember the exact moment when I first glimpsed her in the bar while battling the troll. It felt like it lasted forever although it was only a flash.

"And I followed those guys to the warehouse. I knew there was some bad shit going down and that Charleston, and the world, was in danger, but I didn't know what to expect or what was happening. I moved into the abandoned hotel." I laughed. "I thought it was the greatest thing ever after all the time I spent in The Deep."

"I'll point out that I did offer for you to stay in my

house," Ally reminded me. "You didn't have to become one with the mildew and dust."

"And I appreciated it, but I couldn't put you in that kind of danger. I still had no idea what was going on or what would happen next. What I did know was that the Guild would be after my ass, and they would have no problem mowing down whoever was anywhere near me when they found me. I didn't want that to be you. We had barely reunited. I wasn't about to let you become a visual aid in the story of why I'd been missing for ten years. Besides, if I hadn't been at the hotel, I wouldn't have found Dog."

I glanced across the room at him.

"And you saved me from the group of punks," he replied with a slight twitch of his mouth I would have liked to think was a smile if I didn't know better.

"I wasn't going to bring that up, but yes. And you thanked me by scaring the living shit out of me. Thank you for that, by the way."

"You missed a few steps there," Ally interjected. "Remember, we didn't know about Dog until after we went back to the warehouse."

"That's when you found me," Archie added. "Or what was left of me, as it were."

"Yes. And Bentham." I gestured at her. "Of course, she and Thrash were beating the hell out of you at the time, so it wasn't exactly a touching reunion."

"I'm sorry about that, by the way." Bentham leaned forward so she could look at Archie. "Can you take solace in knowing I was only doing my job?"

He waved her off. "It happens. A hazard of dealing in black market Farstuff. It wasn't the first time it happened.

Not even the first time it happened with you. Hopefully, it will be the last, now that we're in the same posse. We *are* in the same posse now, right?"

Bentham gave a short laugh. It was still odd to hear any type of positive or even positive-adjacent emotion come from her.

"I don't know if this counts as a 'posse,' but whatever this is, I'm in it. And I promise I won't try to knock any more of your teeth out." Archie smiled widely. "Unless you piss me off." The smile dropped, and his heavy eyes looked at me imploringly.

"What? I agree with her." I snickered. Bentham laughed again, and it still felt weird to hear it. I would have to get used to it, assuming we made it through this.

"Then we went to that barn out in the middle of nowhere," Ally continued, undaunted by the interruption. "I still had no idea what was going on, and we fought that scary-ass angel."

She sounded almost amused as she reminisced about the earliest days of us being back together. Amused, and surprised, perhaps at being able to compartmentalize such an unbelievable moment.

I remembered the terrifying encounter. "Yeah, that thing isn't ending up on the top of my Christmas tree any time soon."

"It all led up to Folly Beach." Archie eyed Ally as she carefully sewed up a slice on his arm. "That was the strike Hobbes warned about."

I shuddered at the memory of the dead rising from the shipwreck and coming into the crowd. I swore to myself right then and there that I would never watch another nautical-themed ghost or zombie movie as long as I lived.

"But it was only the beginning. It led up to this." I drew a breath and shook my head. "I thought staying away from my family would be enough to protect them, but it's not. Now that I know about my mother and Rand, I'm terrified to leave them alone."

"What do you want to do?" Bentham asked.

"I'm not sure yet. Mostly because we don't know what Rand's next move is. And we still don't know what this is about or why she's obsessed with my family. I know Rand grew up next to my mother, but Dad said she invited her to her birthday party to be nice to her.

"She wouldn't do something like that after bullying her, and she wasn't the type of person to be mean to someone like that, anyway. Besides, after the party, nobody knows what happened to Ayn Adams. I mean, we do. She became Rand, then Hobbes. It's a whole sequence of identities with that one."

"What I don't understand is why she would be there in the first place. I can't imagine the suburbs of Charleston have a huge Farsider population. Especially Philosophers," Ally said.

Bentham nodded. "It would be extremely odd to raise a Philosopher among humans. Respectable ones, at least. It's practically a scandal that the highest-ranking Guild member lived here. Something went seriously wrong."

"And then wrong again," I added. "Because she didn't stay here."

"Something must have happened," Archie jumped in.

"Something that changed awkward little Ayn into the mighty Rand. The origin of the beast."

"Are you saying my mother is *the* reason Rand became a murderous psychopath?"

"Not her specifically, but something happened during that time," he pointed out. "If we can figure that out, we might be closer to knowing what's going on."

We sat quietly for a moment and let Archie's words sink in. They felt right, like we'd cracked a code that had held us back for months.

"I'll look into her human life," Ally volunteered. "I'll see what I can find out from our parents and some of their friends who might remember Ayn."

"Good," I told her. "See if you can find any of her teachers or the principal from the high school around the time she would have gone there. Find out anything you can about her."

"I've already reached out to the Farsiders I can trust, but there are some I still have some leverage over who I can contact," Bentham informed us. "I'll talk to all of them and see what they know about Rand's rise to power. Maybe I can get some insight into her life before the Guild and how she got as powerful as she is."

"Perfect," I agreed. "Archie, can you find somewhere safe to take my family? A spot where they can stay until all this is over?"

"Absolutely," he confirmed.

I nodded and looked at Dog. "You're with me. Until he can find somewhere for them to stay safe while we take down Hobbes, we have to keep an eye on my family." He nodded, and I drew a breath. "All right. You guys try to get a few hours of sleep. The forecast calls for a shitstorm, and we have some sandbags to put in place. Dog and I will head out now. If they come for my family tonight, they're going to catch these hands. And Dog's hands. Paws?"

"Hands." He laughed.

"Hands," I confirmed. "And maybe a knife or two." We headed out into the night, knowing that in the morning, Bentham was off on her errand and the rest would head our way. If I knew Ally, they would be up before the sun, and she would have them barreling our way, ready for war, by four AM. If war happened before that, well, I had Dog.

Something told me that might be enough.

CHAPTER TWENTY-THREE

"Shouldn't wear my sunglasses at night, because I can't see shit," I sang under my breath as Dog and I stood in the shadows on the edge of my family's yard.

I took off my glasses and put them in my pocket, then went back to aimlessly wandering back and forth.

We'd been standing there for a few hours, watching and waiting, but we didn't know for what. That made it worse. We weren't bracing for a specific threat. We didn't know what might happen. All we had to go on was the knowledge that my family was in danger, and I needed to protect them.

It created tension and anxiety, but also made the minutes drag on slowly. Dog stood stiff in the shadows beside me, his eyes the only thing about him that moved as he swept them back and forth across the yard. Were it not for Archie's rune, he wouldn't be in his human form since the full moon wasn't at its peak.

If anything came out of the darkness to go for my family, it wouldn't get past those eyes. They were intensely attentive in a way that sliced through the air and latched onto anything that shifted even the slightest bit. I didn't doubt that if he sensed anything that concerned him at all, he would attack first and ask questions later. It made me hope none of my sisters took after me and would try to sneak back into the house in the next few hours.

These thoughts brought my mind back to the last night I was at home. I'd skipped a concert. Been the "good girl." Gave up everything, or so I thought, for the kids and my family. I couldn't imagine anything worse in the world than my Dad being upset with me. I had no way of knowing that things could be so much worse and would be in a matter of minutes.

I turned from the slice of moonlight that reminded me of my path that night and glanced at Dog again.

"Do you remember the first time I saw you? That night when I was at the back door?" I looked at the door, almost able to envision myself standing there. "I felt you watching me. Does that make sense? I was so worried about getting inside before Dad caught me. I hurried, but I felt something looking at me as I stood there, and when I turned, you were there. Of course, I didn't know it was you.

"All I saw was a big, black dog standing in the shadows. It shouldn't have struck me as much as it did. Some of the neighbors had dogs, and they would get out occasionally and roam around. But when I saw you, something stopped me. Do you think maybe I knew there was something different about you? I don't know how I would have, but maybe?"

I turned back to him and gasped. He was right behind

me and stared at me with his deep, dark eyes as he turned the rune in his hand over and over.

"I'll never forget that night. And I don't know if you might have known something, but I wouldn't put it past you. I wouldn't put anything past the mighty Sara Slick."

I drew in a breath and tried to calm the sudden uptick in my heartbeat. "Thank you."

There was a slight sound near the house, and I went on defense, ready to act in an instant if I needed to. I was primed to run when I noticed movement and a new sliver of light near the roof. We moved back into deeper shadows as my father appeared at the newly opened window.

He leaned his head out for a second, seeming to draw in a deep breath of the fresh air. I stepped slightly forward as he disappeared back into the house. I didn't want him to see me, but it was like that one little glimpse wasn't enough, and him withdrawing dragged me toward him involuntarily. I stopped myself before I went too far onto the lawn.

"Is that the first time you've seen him?"

"Yes." I nodded. "I heard his voice when I was here with Ally, but I haven't seen him since the night I was arrested and brought to The Deep. The last time I saw him, he was sitting in his recliner in the living room getting the hell beaten out of him by Guild Agents.

"One of them pulled out this massive sword made out of ice. It was the scariest thing I'd ever seen. I didn't know what was going on or if it was real, but I couldn't let them do that to him. They didn't know I was there, but I jumped out and stopped them."

"You could have run. You could have saved yourself when you saw how much danger there was."

I glanced at him and shook my head.

"No. I couldn't have. It didn't even cross my mind. My father was right there, and they were threatening him. They accused him of horrible things, and all I could think was they were going to take him away, and it would destroy the entire family. My mother's death had been hard enough for all of us. Not having Dad would not only devastate us, but it would also break our family apart. I was only fifteen. There was no way the authorities would let me raise four little girls on my own. And where would I get the money? How would I keep a roof over their heads or feed them? They needed Dad, and I figured it all had to be some sort of misunderstanding they would sort out.

"I thought they might take me in and I'd be home in a few hours, maybe the next day. I'd get a good story, some street cred, and Dad wouldn't be able to ground me after I flung myself in front of Special Agents to protect him."

"When did you realize that wasn't going to happen?"

"When they didn't walk me out the front door but used a key to open a hole in the fucking fabric of reality and yanked me through it. That was a pretty good clue. Then when I got in The Deep, I still tried to keep it together, but it didn't take long for them to make it super clear I wasn't getting a fair and speedy trial."

"I don't know if I would have held it together as well. Knowing my father, he would have done something to deserve it." He let out a small laugh. "He was a trouble-maker. Runs in the family."

"Ten years I sat stewing in The Deep, and that thought

didn't cross my mind. Not once. Never for an instant. He's not the kind of man to do something horrible enough to justify the things they were saying about him. Besides, nobody seemed to question me being in prison for these crimes. If they were so sure it was my father, I think they would have noticed the slight difference between him and me."

"You think they always knew you didn't do anything?"

"Rand clearly knew. I think most people believed I did, but that's because she made them. She created this whole thing and put me in the position of being a vicious mass murderer and supervillain. I have to say that it went perfectly. She tossed me into the most disgusting hellhole ever crafted in the history of existence for ten years."

I looked at the house again and felt a familiar pang in my heart. "I miss them so much. All of them. My father, my sisters. I can't believe they've grown up without me. The fact that I'm so worried about them and so scared something will happen to them, and I can't go in there and tell them is killing me. I wish we could be together again."

"I'm sorry."

I looked at him again and saw the emotion etched across his face. "I know you miss your pack."

He nodded. "Every day. I've been so lonely since losing them. There were many times the only thing that kept me going was wanting vengeance for them. I never thought I would feel anything close to a bond again."

He paused and his lips curled up slightly. "But then I met you. Being with you and the team has made me feel like I've found a family again."

Dog stepped slightly closer, and my breath caught in

my throat at the heat of his body near mine. Our eyes met, and I felt a strong draw to him. I licked my lips as my heart thudded in my chest. It was a new tension building between us, but it shattered in an instant as a monstrous form crashed through the hedges toward us.

CHAPTER TWENTY-FOUR

Thrash burst through the hedges like a hound on the hunt, and Mill arrived behind us panting in anticipation. Dog and I immediately went back-to-back. Mill sported a vest over his chest that covered where Bentham had hit him with her magic blast, and it looked like he might have a limp to go along with the chip on his shoulder.

This would be bad.

They had magic, and where they were, other Philosophers were likely to follow. Dog and I had, well, fists. Fists and some Archie runes, but that wasn't enough to even the score. Only one thing would help in this situation, but thankfully, I had that in spades.

Rage.

It was almost calming. A feeling of pure, unmitigated hatred washed over me and filled every pore with the fire of a thousand suns. It imbued me with an energy I could only describe as manic, and my fingers twitched in anticipation.

More than kill them, more than stop them, I wanted to

hurt them. I wanted to be hurt. I wanted to feel the pain of battle with them and overcome it. To use that pain to issue it back to them tenfold. I wanted blood.

Dog charged Thrash, and I dove at Mill. There was no plan, no finesse, or discipline. It was a fight. All-out war.

Mill blinked first and drew back his right hand. I drop-kicked his shoulder, and we both hit the ground. I got up and saw he'd formed a magic blast, and ducked in time for it to sail over my head.

I stood straight, intending to throw a jab to take him off his game, but met a fist to my stomach. His arms were like tree trunks and his fists, each the size of a large pizza, covered my entire abdomen. I folded over it, suddenly unable to breathe.

As I crumpled, he raised his boot and crushed it into the side of my face. I felt a tooth go loose and the warm rush of blood in my mouth as the momentum simultaneously spun me and pushed me away. I was dizzy, but I felt no pain.

I was too full of righteous anger to feel that. He pulled his hand back for another magical blast and instead of ducking away, I stood my ground. I wanted to take his best shot. To absorb the fire and the flame and the sonic whatever, even if it was only so I could turn and spit blood in his eye.

The blast hit me square in the chest and knocked me back several feet. It burned like acid on my skin, and for a moment, I couldn't move my fingers. My ribs felt like a baseball bat had walloped them, and it was hard to draw a breath, but I quickly rolled to my stomach and put my knee below me to gain a sense of balance.

I shot a look back at him, and our eyes met, mine full of fire and his full of disbelief.

"Is that all you got? Come on, hit me again, you dick," I shouted.

In my peripheral vision, I saw other Guild Agents crowding around. The Philosophers made a wall around the house and blocked anyone from seeing the war going on in my family's front yard. Inside the house, I saw curtains flicker. They were looking outside and seeing something, and I wondered if they saw me and recognized me.

Then the thought hit me that they were in terrible danger. I had to win for them to live. Pissed and confused, Mill worked up another magical blast and roared as he shot it at me. This time, I sidestepped it and let it explode into a hapless Philosopher who obviously wasn't promoted because of his brains. I reached behind me for the familiar grip of my switchblade and grinned.

"Eat this." I spun into a throwing motion. It was something Solon taught me long ago. A move that in lesser concentration would ensure a missed shot, but with proper motivation and focus, would add to the throwing power and confuse the target. I had the appropriate motivation, and that gave me the focus. I loosed the blade, and it soared through the air.

The ground exploded in front of me before the blade hit, and Mill soared out of range. Dog had used the sonic whip. The ancient tree that had been my way inside since teenagerhood cracked. Mill stumbled as he tried to stand, and my switchblade buried itself in the tree.

I had no time to waste. I ran as fast as I could, trying to

maintain balance on the still-rumbling ground and leapt into the air. I crashed down foot-first onto the bridge of his nose. The crack of bones was audible, and his hand instinctively went up as blood poured out. It oozed between his fingers in clumps and into his mouth.

I reared back and soccer-kicked him in the ribs. He was huge and muscular, but breathing was essential, and those bones were easy to break if you knew how to hit them. I repeated the kick, then knelt close to him. He was in pain and surprised, but my anger was overwhelming. I could end him right here, right now, but I needed to make it hurt. I wanted him to spend his last few seconds wondering when Sara Slick would finish.

And I wanted all the Farsiders watching to know fear.

I fired an elbow into his jaw and felt it loosen under the shot. If I hadn't broken it, I'd dislocated it. I balled up a fist and smashed it into the jawbone, making sure to hit it at the right angle that pushed the teeth together with a hard clack, likely breaking one or more. His eyes glazed over, and I realized if I kept hitting him, he would go unconscious.

Not today.

I stood and walked over to the tree. The knife wrenched loose with a hard tug, and I turned to face Thrash. Unfortunately for me, he was already in the air, fist glowing and pulled back. I had a fraction of a second to respond. I pulled back, which kept the punch from knocking me out or maybe killing me, but not much else. I flew backward and landed hard on my hip.

My cheek burned and sizzled from the blow, and I tried to shake the cobwebs out fast enough to get to my feet before he could do it again. As I rose to my knees, I caught something rushing toward me out of the side of my eye. My stomach sank as I looked up to see Mill's massive frame bearing down on me. I was still so rattled from the Thrash punch that I wouldn't be able to block whatever he had in store.

Part of me wanted to close my eyes and wince before he got there, but I refused. I wanted to look my killer dead in the eyes.

His arm raised, and I waited for the blow that would surely end my existence. His muscles flexed, and the limb hurtled toward me, then everything seemed to slow down. As if in slow motion, I watched as Dog's blurred form entered my field of vision. He tackled Mill, and the arm of doom that was coming for me fell limply away as they careened to the side.

As if someone hit the play button, normal time resumed, and I let out a breath I didn't know I'd held. I searched around me for the knife, which had flown from my hand when Thrash smashed me.

I saw it lying a few yards away and scrambled toward it on my stomach. I looked up to see Philosophers lying everywhere. Between Dog using the sonic whip and missed blasts from Thrash and Mill, it looked like they had taken out most of their backup. We might get through this.

It was possible to win.

My fingers seized the switchblade, and I got to my knees and elbows when something hit me. I didn't see Thrash. I looked again and saw bodies everywhere, but Thrash wasn't among them. Then I heard a sound that made my stomach drop. There was a crash, a thumping sound, and a scream inside the house. I ran toward the front of the building fast enough to see Thrash, and his elongated limbs stretched as he ran.

My little sister dangled from his freakish arms.

He had taken Mia.

CHAPTER TWENTY-FIVE

It took me a second to process what I saw. It didn't make sense. It was too awful, too gut-wrenching for me to want to accept it was happening. But reality hit me like a truck barreling down the highway, and I couldn't stand there in the yard waiting for it to change.

Thrash had Mia. The monstrous creature with the blood of countless Far and Near people on his hands had snatched up my sister and run away with her.

It felt like the two worlds of my existence, The Near where I was born and The Far where I grew up and learned the truth, crashed together. It was more than having Ally along with me for my fight against Hobbes. It was more than having Archie and Dog as part of my life. It was more than the night I watched the guards attack my father before they took me.

Seeing Thrash running away from the house with Mia in his arms was the two halves of myself smashing together in a way I never wanted them to.

Coming here was supposed to be about protecting

them. I was supposed to stand guard outside the house and keep anything from happening to them until Archie found a place he knew they would be safe. That was the only thing that would make this situation even close to okay.

The war was coming. Fuck that. It was here. It had already begun, and it would only get much worse. The only way I could fight with a clear mind was to know my family was safe. But I'd failed them. They had my sister.

Which meant they had to deal with me.

I took off after Thrash, not caring who might see us. It didn't matter anymore. With the battle that had played out around the house, it was safe to say the jig was pretty well up. At this point, everybody in the neighborhood either knew something serious was going on, or they thought there was some tremendously dedicated experimental theater happening. It didn't matter who saw me or any of the others.

I would get Mia back.

It turned out there was no such thing as a home-field advantage when it came to chasing Thrash. He seemed to know exactly where he was going, and no matter how hard I pushed myself, he was a fast son of a bitch. I couldn't seem to close the space between us. We got into the woods, and he wove through the trees, steadily going farther into the darkness.

Mia bounced in his arms as she struggled against him and screamed. Her voice reverberated around me, and the sound cut into me and made my stomach turn.

I was too familiar with screams of terror and pain. They were most of what I had heard for ten long years. When I was in The Deep, I learned to shove them into the back of my mind. I compartmentalized them so I didn't have to think about what they were or what they meant. That was impossible now. Nothing could make me not realize that was my terrified and confused sister screaming for help she didn't know was coming.

Seeing her grown hadn't changed my thoughts about Mia. I knew in the logical part of my mind—the part that understood time still passed and things changed when I wasn't there, the part that saw the teenage girl and realized it was Mia—that she had grown up. But the rest of me wouldn't accept it.

To me, she was still my little sister who was only six years old the night I was taken from her. When Thrash grabbed her, he grabbed that little girl who I wasn't able to protect. Now I would protect her if it meant laying down my life.

Ahead of me, Thrash took a sudden sharp turn. When I got to the point where he disappeared, I couldn't find him. "Shit!" I shouted.

I didn't know what to do. Panic rose in my throat and made my mind spin. He could be anywhere and doing anything to her. Just because I took his key from him didn't mean he didn't have another one. He had traveled from The Far to here, so he could easily use the key and be out of my grasp.

Sounds behind me made me turn sharply. I hoped he was playing a screwed up game of hide-and-seek and lurked behind one of the trees so he could confront me one-on-one. That would have been fine with me. I would happily look him in the eye and do everything I could to take him down. Instead, I saw Dog.

He was pulling off clothes as he came toward me. I did my best not to stare at him. The amulet bounced against his chest as he rifled through the bag he brought along for a cleaner, less bloodied shirt. By the time he reached me, he had pulled on a tight black shirt that showed off his muscular chest and arms.

"Dressing for the occasion?" Dog usually went buck-ass naked into a change.

"It should help protect the wounds," he informed me. I nodded. This wasn't the time for the things I wanted to say.

He removed the amulet and tucked it in the bag before he handed it to me without a word and headed deeper into the woods. I watched as his form melted into a hulking animal with his nose to the ground. He sniffed for a few seconds to orient himself and figure out what he was working with before he ran off.

I slung the bag over my shoulder and fell into step behind him. Flashes of him were visible between the trees as he ran, but they grew smaller and less noticeable the further we went into the woods. Darkness pressed in around me until the only thing I had to follow was the sound of his paws cracking twigs and breaking through the underbrush.

There were other sounds—footsteps and the rush of branches and leaves moving out of the way to either side of me, but I did my best to ignore them. I couldn't think about who or what else might be in the woods. The only thing I could concentrate on was following Dog and getting to Thrash.

My lungs burned as I ran harder and faster. Despite how much my physical condition had strengthened, and my endurance increased over the last several months, it was still a challenge to manage the terrain of the woods in the dark. I tried to put myself back in the years when I was a little girl and used to play back here. My father didn't like it. He thought it was too dangerous for me to run around alone.

He had no idea the kinds of dangers I would end up encountering among the trees.

It felt like I'd been running for hours when I finally saw the trees start to thin ahead of me. The sound of Dog's paws disappeared, and I had only the moonlight coming down in what had to be a clearing to guide me. As I drew closer, I realized what I thought were the night calls of insects in the woods were voices. A startling number of them.

Something caught the toe of my boot, and I tumbled out of the trees and into the clearing. The ground went from the soft, damp soil and dead leaves of the forest to something hard, and I looked down to see the remnants of a cracked, overgrown parking lot beneath my feet. I glanced back and saw that I'd tripped over a chunk of old, worn concrete at the edge of the lot.

But neither of those things mattered much. What had my attention was the old, abandoned warehouse several hundred feet away. Whatever company once owned the place had closed shop decades ago. I never knew this place existed, but the Farsiders did. At least, they did now. Dozens of them surrounded the warehouse, seeming to come from all sides. I did the only thing there was to do.

I ran toward them.

A new jolt of energy brought on by seeing the swarm of

baddies carried my feet across the lot in seconds. I charged toward the mass of creatures, heading directly for where I saw Dog in their midst. His thick fur stood on end as he snarled at a troll coming toward him.

He was so focused on the drooling, grotesque creature in front of him that he didn't notice the goblin approaching from the side. I launched at him and knocked short and nasty out of the way, then pummeled his disgusting pointy face until he didn't move anymore.

I rose from the muck in time to see Dog sink his teeth into the troll's throat. When he pulled away from him, we met eyes and pushed on toward the warehouse. The Farsiders swarmed around us, madder and more numerous by the second as they came at us with fury in their eyes.

The sheer volume and diversity of the group were almost unfathomable, and I knew it was too much for me to handle. But I didn't care. Dog was with me. I could do anything if I knew he was right there beside me.

The warehouse was close enough for me to see the door, and I started toward it. I'd only taken a few steps when I sensed something was wrong. I couldn't tell what it was, but there was a prickling feeling in my brain, and my skin broke out into goosebumps.

I opened my mouth to yell to Dog. I wanted to scream that it was a trap and we needed to go. But the words caught in my throat as I felt a powerful blast hit me in the back and the back of my head.

I dropped to the ground, dazed, and scrambled to get back to my knees. I tasted blood in the back of my mouth as I reached toward where I'd last seen Dog.

"Whu—wait," I croaked. The light dimmed, and I felt myself slipping into unconsciousness.

Not now.

I tried to focus on what little I could see as my vision blurred and things faded away. A shape formed in front of me. I willed myself to focus on it. As the forms swirling around in my vision slowed and settled on one face, I gasped, and my heart sank. Bentham knelt in front of me and looked at me nervously.

"Why…" I managed, but the sound of screeching tires cut me off right before a van drove through the crowd. It knocked Farsiders out of the way and crushed a few beneath its tires. The door opened, and Bentham yanked me up off the ground, tossed me in, then scrambled up and tackled me to the floor. I heard the door slam closed before the van launched away.

CHAPTER TWENTY-SIX

I tried to shove myself up from the floor of the van and buck Bentham off me, but she had me pinned. My lips burned as they scraped across the carpet while I screamed and cussed. Rage coursed through me and made heat rush along my veins and sting on my skin.

"Get the fuck off me!" I screamed.

Bentham spoke to somebody, but the position she was in meant her arms were pressed to either side of my head and muffled the sound. Combined with my blood rushing in my ears and the thump of my racing heart, I couldn't tell what she said or how many other people were in the van with us.

Finally, I gathered all the strength and energy I had to push back against Bentham's weight on top of me. The force was enough, and she toppled back. As soon as I could move, I jumped up and turned to thrash her.

A hand on the back of my shirt dragged me backward, and I fought and struggled against it.

"What the hell, Bentham? I trusted you! What the fuck are you doing?" I shouted.

The hand behind me gave another hard yank, and I realized there was an extra layer of pressure restraining me. It distracted me long enough to recognize a voice saying my name. It cut through the fog of rage and forced me to think more clearly.

"Slick! Slick, listen to me," Ally called. "It's okay. Chill out."

Ally? Was that seriously Ally's voice? What in the picked at the peak of freshness and flash-frozen hell was going on here? The last I knew, Ally was going to dig into Rand's human life and try to find out as much as she could about her when she still went by the name Ayn Adams.

She was on research, not kidnapping. But now she drove the van with one hand and yanked me backward across it and away from Bentham with the other. Was she in on this? Was she teaming up with Bentham to feed me to the Guild?

Was she seriously that hard-up for things to write about and desperate for fame as a paranormal journalist? That was fucked up.

I realized the other level of pressure pulling me back to help Ally was Dog's teeth. This had reached epically not acceptable levels. Nearly my entire team had turned against me. If the glove compartment popped open and Archie unfolded himself from it to stab me in the neck with a sedative or something, I would be seriously pissed.

Splinter scrambled out of my pocket and rushed up my chest and over my shoulder. He bared his teeth, but before he could bite, Ally shook her head.

"No. It's okay. Seriously. Both of you calm down. We aren't kidnapping you."

"I think that's exactly what you're doing," I argued.

"We're saving you," Bentham corrected.

"Saving me?" I shouted. "By blasting me when I wasn't looking and throwing me in a van?"

Despite the ridiculousness of the situation, I forced myself to settle down so I could hear what they had to say. There weren't a lot of other choices. Even if I were willing to toss myself out of the van and take my chances with a tuck and roll, I didn't have that option. Ally knew me too well and had deployed the child lock so I couldn't open the back door.

"Yes." She put both hands on the wheel and took a turn sharp enough to knock me over. "Bentham was trying to save your life. There was no way you would survive that fight."

"But my sister," I argued. "Mia is in there somewhere."

"I know," Bentham cut in. "I know she is. And I understand that's scary for you. But I know Thrash. He doesn't care about your sister. That's not the point of him being on this assignment. He's a powerful fighter but has a very one-track mind. He does what he's sent to do, and that's the same thing he's doing now. He didn't take your sister to hurt her. He only cares about killing you. She's the bait."

"Bait?"

"Yes. He knew you were at your family's house to protect them, which means the most important thing to you is your family. The easiest way to get you where they wanted you was to take one of them and lure you to the warehouse. You, being the jackass hero you are, did exactly what they wanted you to do. And because Dog won't let you do anything without him there to help you, he flew off to hunt them down, too," Bentham pointed out.

"And if we hadn't stopped you and you ran in there all half-cocked, you would have died, then Dog would have died, and they would have killed your sister in celebration of both of you being dead," Ally added. "You would have gone flailing into the warehouse and been dead in about twelve seconds. Did you see how many Farsiders were there? That was a freaking Harbinger convention."

"You only have one chance of saving Mia," Bentham told me before I could respond. "It's not hopeless. Right now, she's still all right."

"She's with Thrash, in an abandoned warehouse that looked like when it was operational it manufactured doom and misery, and surrounded by every type of Far-slime I've ever seen, and a few I haven't. I don't think right now is the point to say she's all right," I screamed.

"She's alive," Bentham quickly amended. "She's alive, and I doubt she's hurt in any way. They want to keep her useful, and that means she needs to stay in good condition until she does her job. You can still save her. But you only have one chance, and you can't do it alone."

"So, we came and scooped you up before you could ruin everything," Ally said.

"Wow. Thanks for the resounding endorsement." I said flatly.

I wanted to argue my point, but everything they said made sense. When I saw Thrash running away with my sister in his arms, all I could think about was getting her back. I didn't give myself the chance to think through everything. The truth was, they didn't have any use for Mia.

She didn't know anything and couldn't do anything either for or against them. The recent attacks had taken many human lives but not individually. It wouldn't do them any good to kill her. They didn't want her.

They wanted me.

I drew a few breaths to force myself to calm down further. Finally, my body relaxed, and my heartbeat returned to normal. Worry still made the tendons down the back of my neck tight and painful and twisted my stomach into a knot, but I knew the only way I would get Mia back was to listen to them. Bentham was right. I couldn't do this on my own. I needed my collection of merry misfits.

"So, what's our play? What do we do next?" I asked.

"We need more guns. Both figuratively and literally," Bentham replied. "What we have won't be enough." Splinter glared at her, and she looked at him with about as much tenderness as I thought she could probably gather. "You are wonderful, and I know you will always be there to defend Slick. But this is bigger than that. It's bigger than all of us. We need as much power and as much force as we can gather."

That placated him, and he hopped down to curl into my pocket again.

Ally added, "There's also something you need to see."

CHAPTER TWENTY-SEVEN

"What do you need to show me?"

"Hold on. We need to find somewhere to stop," Ally replied.

That was the first time I bothered to pay attention to where we were. I couldn't see through the deeply tinted van windows, but pulling myself up onto my knees and turning to look through the windshield gave me more perspective.

I no longer saw the horde of creatures that swarmed around the warehouse. Instead, the van rocketed down a dark, narrow access road.

"In all the time I lived in Charleston, I never knew any of this was back here."

"You didn't?" Ally sounded surprised.

"Is there some reason I should have?"

"It was a pretty popular place for dares for a while. Kids challenged each other to go out there at night and spend an hour in there without their phones."

"Ally...was I in The Deep at the time?"

She paused.

"Um…maybe."

"Ok. So, we go back to I didn't know this place existed."

"Well, don't get too attached to it. With that many Harbingers crawling around it, it probably won't be there for much longer. Someone will eventually blow it up or light it on fire or something," Bentham pointed out.

"Fair enough," I agreed.

Ally turned off the access road, and we drove a short distance down the highway until we found a rest area. It was dark and deserted, which increased its appeal. If Rand and her posse of the warped and deranged were lying in wait, I wanted as few humans to get swept up in it as possible.

It was hard enough having to battle the Far-scum without throwing in the added pressure of protecting humans at the same time. It was like a far more complicated and potentially upsetting version of the carnival game where you're supposed to shoot at the little targets as they go by, but avoid the cute ducks, or they make a horrible sound and fall over.

Unprepared humans in these battles made horrible sounds and fell over, but there was a lot more at stake than a giant stuffed banana wearing a fruit hat.

Ally drove to a corner of the lot, backed into a spot, and parked. Dog scratched at the sliding door and Ally let him out, where he immediately went on patrol. Ally then climbed into the back with us and settled on the floor.

It was a sobering realization that a large percentage of the time I had been in moving vehicles in the last ten years was in cargo vans. That seemed to say something about my life and its direction.

Once settled, Ally reached under the front seat and pulled out a thick black leather messenger bag. She flipped it open and pulled out several file folders.

"So, I told you I was going to dig into Rand and find out what her life was like when she was doing the human thing."

"Yeah." I nodded. "Did you find anything?"

"I did. A lot." Ally was pleased. "Looking into the life of the young Ayn Adams was nowhere near as difficult as I had prepared myself for it to be. It was like looking into any other human."

"Which means the Guild didn't try to cover it up," I mused. "That surprises me. Wouldn't it be somewhat of a source of embarrassment for them for their most powerful Philosopher to have grown up in The Near? Tainted by Near-gross and whatnot?"

"It would if they knew about it. But for that to happen, Rand would have to tell them, and there's no way she would do that. It would endanger her rise to power, and it would humiliate her. Not only because of the time she spent there, but because of why she was there," Bentham explained.

"I don't think I follow you," I said.

Ally opened one of the files and sifted through the papers.

"Part of researching the young Ayn Adams was finding out about her family. Where she came from and if she always lived beside your mother, that sort of thing. Well, as

I dug into that, I came across what I think is a valuable bit of information."

She handed me a document. I looked down at it and saw it was a scanned copy of a birth certificate.

"Her birth certificate? Your valuable bit of information is that Ayn Adams A.K.A. Rand the Pretty Fucking Terrible the First, was born?"

"Not exactly. If you do a quick scan, you'll find a detail even your father didn't know. He was able to tell us Rand's name and told me her mother's name was Marie Adams. But what he couldn't tell me was Ayn's father's name. He was absent. No one had ever met him, didn't know who he was, and she never talked about him. It seems he wasn't a mystery, though. Mrs. Adams put him right there on the birth certificate."

My eyes ran down the page until I got to the name of her absent father. A ripple of shock went through me.

"Michael Solon," I read.

"Slick, do you know why Solon was in The Deep?" Bentham asked.

The mention of my mentor, my dear friend, made my throat tight and I shook my head to get rid of the painful emotion.

"No. He would never tell me. I asked, but he refused to say anything about it. I didn't know anything about his past."

Bentham nodded to acknowledge my level of under-standing and prepare herself for what she had to tell me next.

"There was a time when Solon was a high-ranking member of the Guild. He had a tremendous amount of influence and power. His ways weren't exactly conventional, and he rubbed some people the wrong way, but that didn't change his position. What did was when he decided to have an affair with a human woman."

I gasped, and my eyes snapped to Ally. She nodded, and I looked back at Bentham.

"There's no mixing in The Far."

"To put it lightly," she agreed. "It's explicitly forbidden in the *Pax*. One of the most stringently upheld laws. Being a Guild member made it even more of an egregious infraction. So, they sentenced him to life in The Deep."

"Oh, only one life?" I asked sarcastically. "That's nothing. They threw ten of them at me."

"The patriarchy." Ally shook her head and gave me at least a moment of levity.

"Seeing the certificate got me thinking." Bentham continued past our nonsense. "I got in touch with someone I'm friendly with in The Heights, and they dug up all the records on Rand."

"Someone you're friendly with?" I lifted one eyebrow.

"Focus, Slick." She shook her head. I knew I needed to, but I didn't want to hear the rest. I knew where we were spiraling and didn't want to go there.

She continued, "From what I found out, Rand appeared on the map out of nowhere. She rose through the ranks of the Guild very quickly and showed incredible power from a young age. She was so impressive and immediately influential that she encountered very little if any resistance. But no one knows anything about her before she started that climb. They know nothing about her childhood or where she came from."

"Because her father was sitting in prison rotting away for the relationship that led to her existence," I stated.

Bentham nodded. "That's what it seems. Looking at the years and the timeline, it would mean they arrested Solon when Rand was fairly young. About ten years old. She didn't live next door to your mother until right around that age. Our theory is that Solon had an affair with Marie Adams. When she got pregnant with their child, he knew he couldn't raise her in The Far, so she stayed in The Near with her mother. He visited them clandestinely and maintained as much of a family as he possibly could."

"So, Rand knew. He wasn't an absent father. He was a father who disappeared," I stated.

Ally agreed. "Exactly. She knew him because he was there for the first ten years of her life. He told Marie about who he was and wanted to raise his child to know who and what she was."

"He probably hoped she would be able to go with him to The Far when she grew up." I laughed bitterly. "He wanted her to be proud of who she was."

"Yes. Only he wasn't careful enough. The Guild found out and arrested Solon. They threw him into The Deep without him having the chance to explain things to his daughter. To Rand, he left her in a world she hated. She despised the human world. It's possible he even brought her into The Far once or twice when she was very young so she had some idea of what it was like. He left when she was young enough that it had a tremendous impact on her. She felt abandoned, and it made her hate the human world, and humans, even more," Bentham related.

"What does that have to do with my family?"

"Your mother was a symbol of that world. Marie and Ayn moved into the house next door soon after Solon was arrested. She watched your mother grow up happy and well-adjusted in a perfect human family. Then it was at your mother's party where Ayn received the final torment that pushed her over the edge. Your mother became the ultimate representation of everything she hated about this world and her life. So, she left and became Rand," Bentham concluded.

"Then she became Hobbes," I added.

The radio crackled to life, and Ally rushed to answer the call.

"Do you have her?" Archie asked.

"They successfully stole me," I called to him.

"Perfect," he said. "The big guns are ready."

I met Ally's eyes, and we smiled. Excellent.

"Time to get my sister."

CHAPTER TWENTY-EIGHT

The area outside the warehouse wasn't the same bustling pit of chaos it had been when I first came out of the woods. The horde of Far creatures had either dispersed or, more likely, stuffed themselves inside the building's hulking corpse and were preparing for the next step.

Ally dropped us off on the access road and continued to her position, which meant Bentham and I crossed through part of the parking lot on our way to where we waited now. The path brought us right past where they picked me up hours before, and the torn, battered corpses of the several Farsiders Ally mowed down.

"They didn't pick them up," I muttered as disgust rippled through my body.

It wasn't disgust at the sight of another dead creature. By now, that was far from something that bothered me. My intolerance for death and bodily remains was forced out of me less than a year into my sentence in The Deep. Think of it as extremely intense and effective exposure therapy.

Instead, it was the sheer brutality of them leaving the bodies out in the parking lot like bits of trash that overflowed from a dumpster. In a way, that was an appropriate analogy, but it was still disturbing.

"They have no reason not to," Bentham said. "Hobbes doesn't care about her followers, Harbingers or not. They aren't living beings to her. They're nothing more than flesh and force. Take their ability to do anything for her out of the equation, and there's nothing left but flesh. To her, those bodies are the box gunpowder comes in. Merely packaging."

I looked at her. "You should write children's books. I think you're missing your calling."

We continued to the selected spot and waited. That had become something I did so much I was strongly considering adding it under "special skills" when I finally put together my post-war resume. But it was necessary.

As much as I wanted to do what they specifically warned me against and run into the situation half-cocked, it wasn't an option. We had to handle this carefully and strategically to be successful.

And it had to be successful.

Bentham and I were quiet for a long time. The tension and uneasiness were still there between us. It would take time for that to go away. But the least I could do was try to meet halfway, or at the very least not let my lingering distrust stop me from being a decent person. Being in The Deep for so long had changed me, but I fought hard to maintain my humanity in there. I didn't let it steal all parts of me then, and it wouldn't do that now. Finally, I turned to her.

"I'm sorry for overreacting when you attacked me."

Bentham barked a short laugh. "It's fine. I mean, I've been attacking you unjustly since you escaped from The Deep. You having an impulse reaction isn't exactly unexpected."

I nodded. The silence fell over us again as we continued to wait and watch the warehouse. It was torture to stand there like that. Things were happening right ahead of us. I knew it. Mere yards away across the broken tarmac and ambitious weeds of a long-forgotten parking lot, Hobbes and her minions continued to plot their war against the world.

This was all the cruelty and horror of the book I read about Hobbes coming to reality. It was everything I'd been afraid of from the first time I heard about Hobbes and learned about the plot. It was everything I worried would come down on The Near and the unwitting humans who had no idea they were sharing their existence with a whole host of creatures who would haunt the darkest corners of the greatest nightmares if they caught even a glimpse of them.

And those were the nice ones.

The reality was, humans as a whole were fragile. Narrow-minded and oblivious purely by merit of their species, they didn't know what was happening around them or the danger seething below the surface. They didn't realize every moment of their lives was measured and dangled on a thread because of the power that existed in The Far. It was better that way.

Although the vast majority of Farsiders were perfectly decent, peaceful creatures who could live among the humans without pitching a fit or causing calamities, that wasn't the case with all of them.

There would always be those who hated The Near. There would always be those who hated humans. Any sense of balance between the two realms was preserved only by the agreement put into place, and that, as we were quickly learning, was fragile.

Human ignorance protected them and ensured they could live their lives comfortably and happily. It was an awkward position to be in, as one of the very few humans in the world who knew the truth and could easily see both sides. I understood The Far and the creatures who lived there as well as I possibly could with my limited exposure, and I'd learned to appreciate individual examples of them. But I was also still human and wanted to preserve the Earth and my kind.

Which meant saving it from those who wanted to destroy it. As I stared at the warehouse, discomfort crawled up my spine.

"My sister's life is at stake," I finally said.

Bentham nodded. "I know."

"She's right there. Somewhere in that building, they have her, and it's up to me to save her," I pointed out.

"You can trust me, Slick."

"I don't have a choice."

Bentham nodded with a pained expression on her face. She drew in a breath.

"I know you don't understand, and it's likely nothing I say will make much of a difference to you. Which I can accept. But I need to tell you. I want you to hear it, and I hope you will at least try to hear what I'm saying. Up until very recently, I thought my duty was to the Guild. It's all I ever knew. Being a part of it was a great honor, a fulfillment, a purpose. It was what I was meant to do with my life, and that was where my loyalty had to lie. But then I learned the Guild was fallible. So I changed my thoughts. Instead, I believed my duty was to the *Pax*. If there was corruption within the Guild, the *Pax* still existed and was the ideal we all strived for. But then I realized that didn't seem to make anything better. So, now, here I am."

"Here you are," I affirmed.

She nodded. "I'm not sure what I'm fighting for anymore, but the one thing I do know is I will fight for you."

Our eyes met, and I saw the sincerity in her stare. But there was no time for me to respond. In the next instant, a loud whistle broke the moment, the signal from Ally telling us it was time to take off toward the warehouse.

CHAPTER TWENTY-NINE

We rushed through the door and surprised them. Two Harbingers stood guard on either side, but when Bentham blasted the door open, it smashed into one of them and knocked her out instantly, and blew the other off his feet.

He scrambled to his knees before I could reach him, and his snout folded like an accordion when I put my boot into it with extreme prejudice. Bentham lit up the second floor with fireball-like blasts while I concentrated on keeping her from being attacked.

Two cyclopes made their way toward her, their movements almost in sync. It took me a second to respond because it was so eerie. It was like a master cyclops brain controlling them across The Near and The Far, and activated these two together.

Both, well, ran wasn't the appropriate word. More like hobble-skipped? They hobble-skipped their big, dumb asses in Bentham's direction, and I cut them off before they could get to her.

I'd learned a few things about fighting cyclopes throughout my time. One was that they had incredible strength and getting in their grip was asking for broken bones. Another was they were *incredibly* dumb. One more obvious fact was that on account of having only one eye, their peripheral vision was almost non-existent.

I rolled toward them but off to one side and sprang to my feet when I was nearly beside them. The closest one had no idea what hit him as I slashed his leg with an off-brand lightsaber Archie made for me. He went down in a heap and made only a grunting noise as he fell.

The other paid no attention, simply stepped on his fellow one-eyed monstrosity, and continued on his way. I snuck up behind him, changed to my switchblade, and jumped on his back. I had roughly three seconds before that big dumb brain of his would figure out I was on him and toss me off like I was a booger and he was a ten-year-old boy. I wrapped my arm around his neck for balance and brought the switchblade around, then jammed it directly into his eye.

He screamed and crumpled to the ground. I dove off him, and Bentham blasted him right out of his shoes. The second one was still trying to get up, without the aid of his now-severed leg, but with the amount of blood he was gushing, I figured he wouldn't make it halfway before he bled out. I turned my attention elsewhere and noticed several warthog-looking guys and another blob monster making their way toward me.

"Great," I muttered under my breath. If there was one thing I hated, other than Thrash and Rand, it was fucking blob monsters.

I wiped the blood off the switchblade from habit, which smeared it across the side of my leg instead, and made my way for the warthogs. The blob monster was slower to the fight, partially because of his snail-like sliding movement, and partly because—and this was a guess—he didn't want any. Frankly, the feeling was mutual.

One of the hogs cocked his fist back as I barreled through the air at him, I caught it on the way down, snapped myself around, and used the momentum to arm-drag him across the room. He tumbled to a stop at the foot of the blob monster, and I was already on my feet and attacking his buddy before he realized he was becoming goo-covered.

His buddy was a slightly different kind of warthog Farsider with a garish mohawk on his head and what looked like ritualistic piercings all over what constituted his face. It made him not only ugly as fuck, but shiny too. It also gave me something to yank when I got close enough.

Sure enough, a boot to the stomach and a knee to his face were enough to daze him, and I hooked a finger into one of the rings coming from his nose and yanked. Blood spewed out, and he screamed in surprise and pain. I added to his misery with a knee directly to where I assumed his balls would be, then a headbutt to his chin. The one-two combination seemed to demoralize and incapacitate him long enough that I could focus on the first one again.

Unfortunately for me, the first warthog dude was already on me. He tackled me to the floor and landed a couple of solid shots to my ribs before I knew what was happening. I trapped one arm as it came down and shifted my hips enough to put me on my side instead of underneath him.

I jumped to my feet while grasping his wrist and spun my leg around his arm. I jumped backward as I fell on my back, which snapped his shoulder and made at least that arm useless for the rest of the day. He tried to roll away in pain, but the blob monster blocked his way.

Something was different about this gooey walking bag of putty. The ground smoked where he went, and there was a distinct smell like burnt rubber in the air. The warthog dude screamed and begged the blob monster not to walk over him, but it did anyway, its yellow, beady eyes trained only on me.

As it did, it was as if it swallowed him. Then a muffled cry came from inside the greenish nearly transparent goo. Then it was past him, but I could still see him lying on the ground where the thing had walked over him.

Well, I could see what was left of him, anyway. His torso was completely missing. His burned and charred head was still there, and his legs, which hadn't been touched by the goo, were still in their locked position. But the torso was gone, evaporated by the acidic touch of this malevolent nightmare Jell-O mold.

"Okay," I said to myself as it continued its approach. "How do I kill you?"

"Fire," answered a voice behind me. I instinctively ducked as Bentham shot the thing dead center with a blast of white-hot fire that burned some of the hair on the back of my head for being too close to it. "Fire always does it," she finished.

"Thanks," I muttered and stood. I looked around.

Most of the warehouse was in various stages of utter demolition, and for the most part, if there was a Farsider, they were in shapes ranging from pretty fucking terrible to dead. I was a breath away from noting that fact when a giant, silver bay door opened to the side of us. We both turned to see not only more of them but an entire fucking army of Farsiders.

"Shit," Bentham muttered. She had already used a lot of firepower to knock out the ones in the room. Neither of us expected an entire second wave that was bigger than the first. And we didn't have time for her to recharge.

They attacked, and the resulting fight was brutal. I barely had decapitated one of them or kicked another in their oversized abdomens before a replacement stood in their spot, smashing into me or slicing me with sharp claws. I was bloody, battered, and slowly retreating backward, and Bentham was doing the same.

There were too many of them. They swarmed us from all sides, and the only thing I could think was I had to hold them off. I had to make sure Mia was here before I could do anything else. All I could do now was survive and hope.

Bentham smashed the heads of two Farsiders together and turned to look at me. Her teeth were gritted, and her stance was strong, heroic even. But her eyes were desperate. She knew as well as I did that we were outnumbered and out-weapond. We had to survive, but that might not be as easy as we had hoped.

A fist crunched into my stomach, and I doubled over. Somewhere in the crowd, I heard Bentham cry out in pain too. Claws dug into my thigh, and I kicked a shadowy beast off me. I had to get to my feet, but every time I got close, I would get smashed down again.

Suddenly, the attacks stopped. I was on my stomach, trying to will my arms to get under me again and push me up from the floor. Blood flowed from a wound on my eyebrow and created a stream that connected me to the ground like cheap glue.

I got my knees under me and noticed that the sound in the room had changed. No longer was there the frantic charge of war, but a pensive sound—a waiting one. The Farsiders had been called off by someone who commanded them.

Then I heard the laugh crackle through the air. It broke the tension in the room and filled my heart with rage. My blood boiled and my fingers clenched on the concrete as Thrash's high-pitched giggle seared into my brain like a cleaver. I got to my knees and sat up, my back to the noise, and saw Bentham off to my side, also on the floor although she was on her back.

At first, I had a jolt of fear that she was dead, but she twitched and started to move. Then her face scrunched up into a mask of bloodied disgust. She could see Thrash.

I didn't want to turn around. I didn't want to see his stupid fucking face until I had to. When I turned, it was with reluctance, and even with the pain I was in, it was sheer hatred that kept me from giving him the respect of looking at him directly for as long as I did.

When I finally faced him, our eyes met, but only for a moment. As enamored as he was to have me at his mercy, his wild, piercing eyes darted back to Bentham. She was his prize. His lips curled upward in a toothy, maniacal grin.

When he spoke, it was like gravel in my ears, but nearly musical for Thrash.

"Good to see you again, Bentham." He wiped spittle from one of his lips. His anticipation and excitement made him drool. "This will be fun."

CHAPTER THIRTY

"Search her." Thrash pointed at me as the grin stretched ever wider across his face.

A Farsider with gills on the sides of his cheeks hustled up to me, eager to do Thrash's bidding. He stuffed his hands in my pockets and caught a headbutt to his cheek for it. It was all I had left at the moment, and a vicious left cross put me down long enough for him to fish out my switchblade and a couple of other runes Archie had given me.

"What about her?" snarled a short, squat Harbinger that I could only describe as an angry pile of laundry with a head.

"Bentham wouldn't use runes. She wouldn't lower herself that far. Would you, Bentham?"

There was silence in the room as the two former partners stared at one another.

"I don't need runes to beat you," she finally croaked. She was obviously in tremendous pain, but she had worked her way back up to her elbows again. She looked at me as if she needed confirmation that I was still there, then back at Thrash. "Why don't you fight me one-on-one and I'll show you?"

"You would like that. Maybe I would, too. But I will like what I have planned for you a lot more. You," Thrash ordered the basket of dirty laundry cosplaying as a Farsider, "tie her up. Tie them both up."

Farsiders surrounded us and lifted us. I tried to fight back a little, but a Christmas ham-sized fist to my stomach took the wind, and the fight, out of me pretty quickly. They shoved me onto a plastic chair, and ropes seemed to materialize from the crowd.

Rough hands bound my legs to each leg of the chair, then wrenched my arms behind me and tied them tightly. Bentham was only feet away from me, and I watched as she was tied identically to me with her arms behind her. Our eyes made contact again, and she nodded.

This was going to suck.

"Everyone back away," Thrash shouted, and the Farsiders followed his orders.

He sauntered forward now, obviously feeling like he had won. It made me sick to see how giddy he was. There was nothing redeemable in Thrash, and there had never been. From the beginning, I saw something decent in Bentham. Thrash never had that. He was always an unrepentant jackass.

Thrash walked up to me first. He eyed me in a way that combined every bit of sleaze possible with a hateful delight in violence. He raised his hand as if to backhand me and stopped. I didn't flinch. He paused for a moment, seeming to calculate the merits of hitting me first, then let his hand fly.

It struck me hard across the cheek. I took a moment to embrace the pain, to sit with it and let it fill me with rage again. The anger was the only thing that could override the pain throughout my body. I swiveled my head back to his sickly grinning face and spat blood onto his shirt.

That seemed to wipe the smile off his face. Of course, it replaced it with wide-eyed fury, and he pounded a few shots into my jaw and my stomach. With my hands tied behind me and my legs tied to the chair, I couldn't do anything except absorb the blows.

My head rang, and my vision was blurry when he walked away toward Bentham. I saw two of each of them swimming and occasionally merging into one again before floating away in half circles.

"I always knew you were weak." He leaned close to her ear. "I asked every single day for permission to gut you where you stood. You were lazy and insubordinate, and worst of all, you had mercy. Mercy for Nearsiders. Mercy for Sara Slick. Mercy for the people who got caught up in her little freak show. It made me want to puke."

Bentham struggled against her restraints, and Thrash's grin returned.

"Yet here you are," he said to the room at large, his arms rising to invite them into his conversation.

His theatrical streak was showing now, and he had a captive room to speak to. "Bentham the failure, sitting side by side with little Sara Slick. The two of you look so cute together. Stars of your own little hero story, weren't you? But life isn't a story, Bentham. Life is cruel and vicious. Life is a fucking war, and I won. I beat you, and now I'll enjoy making you bleed. But there is one way to stop me." He leaned close to her ear again, and I barely heard his whisper. "I want you to beg me for your life."

Bentham struggled with renewed vigor, but the Farsiders had gagged her. Her voice rose above the gag as she tried to yell curse words at him that I was sure she was inventing on the spot. Thrash stood straight, and his hand glowed orange. He brought it down hard on her face, and she slumped sideways, her breath heavy and blood trickling out of her nose.

"Feel like a big man?" I spat blood and tried to clear my assuredly broken nose.

"You." He stalked back to me. "You always have something to say. That's why I didn't have them gag you. I want you to talk all you want. In fact, I have someone you can talk to."

He waved at one of the Harbingers, and a door opened. A wheelchair came into view with a person tied, blindfolded, and sagging in it. It was Mia. Tears streamed down her face, but she was awake and seemingly unhurt. It was my turn to receive a personal bubble-bursting whisper session from Thrash.

"For every word you say, I will cut your sister. For every noise you make, I will hit her. For every time I think you're pissing me off by your general demeanor, I will increase my violence on her until I have her on the brink of death. How long do you think that will be?" he hissed. "She isn't a fighter, Slick. She doesn't have your capacity for pain. How long before she begs for her Daddy? How long before she begs to die? I want to know the answers to each of those questions, and I will start with the first fucking peep out of your mouth. Do you understand?"

I stared stone-faced at him, and he pushed his forehead into mine. His breath smelled like spoiled milk and his cologne was overpowering, and even with my nose in the shape it was in, both smells made me nauseous.

"Answer me, dammit." He pushed his forehead harder into mine.

I nodded. It was enough. He stopped pushing, but then his tongue extended, and he licked the blood off my eyebrow. He looked like someone tasting wine as he sloshed it in his mouth. He spat it out at my feet and smiled.

"Good. Now sit here and be a good girl," he muttered, then walked back to Bentham.

Mia didn't know I was here, not unless they told her. And if they had, I figured she would be screaming for me, so my guess was no. She was twenty yards away from me, and I saw the fear in her.

She was terrified and alone, or she thought she was alone. She was me ten years ago. My heart ached for her, and I wanted to shout her name, to tell her it would be okay, that I was here. But Thrash wasn't the kind of person not to make good on a threat he made. One peep…

I kept my mouth shut and turned to Bentham. Her face was a mask of pain, but she was still there. Recognition crossed her face, and I saw her move one arm, twisting it so that it reached as far up as she could manage while she leaned her head back over the back of the chair. Her fingers reached, and I knew what I had to do.

I coughed.

Thrash turned toward me with his eyes ablaze. He was elated. He strode past me toward Mia, and I muttered under my breath.

"You lost."

He stopped cold. One foot was in mid-air, and it slowly lowered to the floor. He turned back to me and got close again.

"That's two cuts and a punch, you know."

"You lost."

"Four cuts, now. Do we want more? Are you going for broke in hopes that I behead her and make it quick? I won't make it quick, Slick. I'm a professional, you see."

"You lost."

"Stop saying that!" he shouted and straightened. "I won. Obviously, I won. And perhaps I should get it over with and gut you right now."

"You fell into my trap," I spat and grinned, if for no other reason than to piss him off. A moment of fear passed through his eyes. Then a shadow dropped over them.

"Your trap? This is my fucking trap. You're the one tied to a chair, and I have your runes. You only want to prolong the night to come up with a plan. I know you, Sara Slick. But this time it won't work, this time—"

"I only needed to make sure my sister was here and safe," I interrupted. "But it helps that you're standing where you're standing. I'll enjoy this."

"Enjoy what?" he began, then his eyes swiveled to Bentham. The rune she had pulled from the necklace dangled in her hand. It was blinking. She tossed it toward us, and I clenched my eyes shut.

The world exploded in light and fire and pain. It blew

me toward a wall, and the chair bent and the plastic broke. One of my legs slid free, and my arms were able to move, the plastic they were tied to no longer in place behind me. Thrash lay moaning a few yards away as Harbingers closed in around us. It was time. I hoped Ally saw the explosion.

Another blast obliterated the opposite wall. Light poured in, quickly darkened by shadows. I squinted and smiled at what I saw. Dog in human form stood at the front of an army.

Lizards and Vrya and a handful of the West Virginian miners mixed and held weapons ranging from rune-based blades and blunt instruments to axes and rifles. Archie, Ally, and Pip were among them. Their eyes scanned the room for me. Ally found me and pointed.

The cavalry had arrived.

CHAPTER THIRTY-ONE

There was utter pandemonium around me, and I struggled to get to my feet. Everything hurt like hell, and I worried that maybe I didn't have enough left in the tank. Perhaps this was the last fight for Sara Slick. If it were, I would get Mia out of here safely first. I could die happy knowing my family was safe.

A Farsider, a long, lithe-looking thing with rings all over its effeminate face and tattoos of a language I didn't recognize covering its masculine body, was feet from me. In its hands was a curved blade, which glinted in the light. Its rubbery limbs reached for me, and I swatted them away with arms that were suddenly free. They ached and burned, but there was still strength left in them.

The hand with the blade swiped back, and I moved my head in time for it to pass inches from my neck. I mustered everything I had left, kicked my legs around, and swept it off its feet so it landed hard on the concrete floor.

I was going to scramble away to get some room, but before I could, Dog leapt into my vision. The Farsider was nearly on its feet again when Dog's feet smashed into its cheeks and sent it barreling toward the wall. Dog got back to his knees, and Ally was already there, rushing to me. I suddenly noticed I was surrounded by Vrya, who had turned into a protective tree-like circle and were battling Farsiders. My vision was still swimmy as I tried to focus on Ally a few feet in front of my face.

"Slick, you look like shit." She rooted around in a bag.

"Yeah, well, bruises heal. I'll be hot again soon."

"Who said you were hot before?" She filled a vial with a dark brown substance that I was sure that I would have to drink and that would taste like hot, roasted ass.

"Lots of people."

Splinter, who had been hiding in Ally's bag, rushed out and jumped on my chest. His spiky hair dug into painful cuts on my cheek and neck, but I nuzzled him anyway.

"See? Splinter thinks I'm all right."

"Here," Ally instructed as she ignored my continued fight for my ego, "you'll want to down this. I have a soda to chase it with."

"It's that bad?" All three of her nodded. I shrugged and took the vial from her, pressed it to my lips, and tilted my head back. It oozed out of the glass instead of poured and took forever to get down my throat. Much like I guessed, it tasted like hot, roasted ass.

When it was finally down, Ally handed me the soda, and I guzzled it. I had only swallowed a few gulps of the bubbly drink when I suddenly felt a rush of adrenaline. I looked down at my hands and noticed them pulsing, and a large gash on my left forearm was mending itself like magic.

"Archie worked that up for you. He said he's working on a mint flavor, but…" Ally explained.

"I don't care how it tastes. It works. Help me up. You need to get to Mia and radio back to me. I have to finish this."

Ally helped me to my feet, and I looked around. In the circle and between where Mia was before the cavalry arrived and me, Thrash struggled to his feet, his face red with rage and surprise, and his eyes wide as he tried to get a handle on the chaos around him. There was little between us now, and he spun to face me. Our eyes met in a moment of recognition. One of us would die, right here, right now. We both knew it. We both were ready for it.

"Get him," a voice behind me said. I didn't need to turn to see who it was. His deep baritone and protective growl gave him away. Dog's hot breath fell on my neck as he spoke. "Finish him off. I'll watch your back."

I nodded and took off. Thrash ran toward me as well. We met in the middle, tackled each other, and fell to the floor. Each of us threw fists into the other's ribs, but I noticed the pain lessened with each shot.

Either he was losing strength, Archie's serum was working overtime or both. I threw an uppercut that seemed to rattle him, and his entire body loosened in my grip. It was time to finish him off, and I pulled back my fist.

Something caught my eye a few feet away. Archie held onto a bag and thrashed wildly at a Farsider who was on the ground and held his leg. It yanked on him, and Archie fell backward, landing hard on the concrete. The Farsider climbed on top of him, and the closest Vrya had his back turned. No one else could help him.

I couldn't hesitate. I had to save Archie right then, or else he was a dead man. I leapt off Thrash, let his mostly limp body fall to the floor, and rolled toward the Farsider, who had snapped a blade into place on his wrist and was raising it. Before he could drive it down, I reached him and planted my boot in his chin.

It was enough to disorient him. I kicked him again and harder, and he fell off Archie and rolled onto his stomach. He got his hands under him and started to stand, but I curb-stomped the back of his head and sent him face-first onto his blade. It came out the back of his skull with a sickening squelch.

Archie had rolled away, and he gave me a look of gratitude. Then his eyes widened, and his hand reached out. Time seemed to slow. I tried to turn, but it was too late. A fist the size of a freight truck hit me like a...well, a freight truck. I fell hard and cracked my head on the concrete. A ringing sound took over my hearing. I tried to look up and saw nothing but a shadow in the size and shape of Thrash.

My mind screamed for my body to get up, to do something, but it was like the message wasn't getting through. I was disoriented and hurt. All I could manage was one hand, reaching up. I didn't have a plan.

Maybe I somehow could grab him or distract him or hurt him with that hand. But he raised his hand too, and his glowed black with a streak of dark red through it. His eyes widened, and his pupils dilated. A laugh bubbled up from his chest, and I saw his body convulse with it, although I couldn't hear it. I grasped lamely at his jacket, and he bared his teeth.

Then he froze. A fist burst through his stomach, then

blood gushed out and rained down around me. The fist glowed an iridescent orange and seemed to vibrate with raw magic. Thrash looked down at it and dropped his hands. His jaw fell wide as he stared at his guts spilling out of his body.

He turned his eyes to me, and I watched the life fade from them. He slumped, and the hand retreated out of him. Another grabbed him by the shoulder and tossed him away like trash. The hands that saved me revealed themselves as my vision slowly focused again, and my fingers tingled as I gained control of them.

Bentham stood before me, her arm soaked in Thrash's blood from the elbow down. Her expression was one of grim determination, with a hint of satisfaction.

She curtly nodded at me and shook guts off her hand. I looked at Thrash's crumpled body and the hole in his stomach that hemorrhaged blood in a wide pool on the ground. His eyes were still open, but lifeless, and turned toward Bentham. She must have been the last thing he ever saw.

Good.

My radio crackled in my ear and Ally's voice came through.

"Slick? Slick, are you listening?"

"I'm here. Thrash is dead."

"The good news keeps on flowing."

"What do you mean?"

"We got Mia," she informed me.

My heart jumped, but I tried to keep myself from feeling too optimistic. Although she said it was good news,

I didn't want to let myself be too happy without knowing what was going on.

"Is she all right?"

"Yes. She's fine. We're bringing her to her family now."

I looked around, took in the victory, and admired the success of us all working together. Suddenly, a laugh bubbled up my throat and out my mouth.

"That's it." The laugh still tumbled around the words.

"What?" Ally asked. "What's going on?"

"I finally figured it out. I know how to beat Rand once and for all."

"How?"

"We give her what she wants."

CHAPTER THIRTY-TWO

My heart ached as I stood in the shadows with Dog and watched Ally lead Mia up the front walk to the front door of my family's house. I wanted more than anything to walk beside them, to be a part of bringing her back safely. I wanted all this to be over so we could be a family again.

Part of me was shocked by the way that thought moved through my mind. It should have been that I wished none of this had ever happened. But that's not how I thought of it anymore.

Not that I ever would have wished for the time I spent in The Deep or what I went through. But now that I had gone through it and knew what I did, I wouldn't change it. Going through that meant I could be here, perched on the edge of saving the world from destruction.

That was worth those years. I would happily lay those ten years down again to know I was defending so many innocent lives and protecting the future.

That didn't mean it wasn't painful to watch my best friend bring my little sister back to my family and try to explain what was going on. They had to be terrified. There was no other way they possibly could have reacted to the chaos and brutality that broke out at the house hours before. I could only imagine how confused and terrified they were. Especially since the police would have no idea what happened and had nothing they could do to help. That was up to us. We had to make sure they were safe, but that meant revealing at least part of the truth to them.

I couldn't hear what Ally was saying, but we'd gone over it several times, so I knew what was happening.

"Mia is all right, but I need you to come with me. I can't get into it right now. There isn't time. All I can say is that it isn't safe here. You need to trust me. We can keep you safe. You need to come with me right now."

I could see my father's face despite the distance. His expression twisted and contorted as he tried to understand what Ally was saying. He was confused and scared, as I expected him to be. It wasn't until that moment that I thought about the night I was taken to The Deep and wondered what my father thought of it.

I always assumed they altered his memory so he wouldn't think of it again, but now I wondered if that were true. Maybe he did remember, although distantly and as if in a dream. Maybe there was still a part of him that remembered the Guild Agents standing over him, and the terrifying sword pulled out of nowhere. If a fragment of those memories existed inside him, he would know how urgent it was to listen to her and follow her instructions.

Whether it was because of those memories or because he trusted her, my father nodded. His expression became resolved, and he turned to my sisters. They all scattered back into the house, and within a few minutes, they reappeared outside, each carrying hastily packed bags. Dad piled my sisters into Ally's van while frantically looking around to detect any threats around the house. Then they drove away.

"They'll be all right," Dog reassured me. "You have to trust that they'll be all right."

"I know." I nodded but didn't take my eyes off the road where the back of the van had disappeared.

Archie walked up to us. He'd arrived at the house before us but stayed on the other side to monitor the perimeter.

"The safe spot I found will be perfect," he reassured me. "It's secure, and they'll have everything they need until this is over."

"I know. I trust you. If I didn't, I wouldn't have had you look for a place for them. It's just hard."

"I know it is," he commiserated. There was something in his voice that made me wonder if there was more meaning to that than merely trying to comfort me. I realized I didn't know a lot about Archie's past. There could be things lurking there he never shared, but that shaped him more than anyone knew. "Here. I brought you something."

He reached into his robes and held out a flat box.

"Is it another rune? Does this one work?"

"One way to find out."

I opened the box and tilted it to let Solon's amulet slide into my palm. My breath caught in my throat as emotion created a hard, painful knot in my chest.

"His amulet," I whispered.

"I fixed it. Sorry it took so long. It's an impressive dyad. It should be perfect now."

I stared at the small piece of unassuming jewelry. It was Solon's first gift to me. It had protected me when I was too weak to do it myself.

"Thank you," I murmured.

"You're welcome."

I threw my arms around Archie for a hug. He tightened up for only a second before he wrapped his arms around me and patted my back. I stepped back from it and looked into his face.

"You gave a real hug," I pointed out.

"I've been practicing," he admitted. "I had Ally bring me a giant teddy bear."

I smiled as warmth spread through my heart. "And you didn't experiment on it to see if you could turn it into a rune?"

Archie shook his head. "It's a teddy bear. It provides strength and protection. As far as I'm concerned, that's already a rune."

"I'm proud of you. You're getting better."

He held his arms out toward me again. "Another one?"

I accepted the hug and smiled as he squeezed me.

"Next thing you know, you'll be going through airport security with abandon," I told him.

Bentham walked up as I wiped away a tear that escaped and tried to focus on the gift Archie gave me.

"Your family is all right?" she asked.

I nodded. "Archie found a place for them, and they're on their way."

"Good. And you? You're sure about this plan?"

I drew in a breath and nodded again. "This is the only way. It has to happen."

There were no protests. The three around me were so different and from diverse walks of life. Up until recently, they lived utterly separate existences and would have no reason to cross each other's path for anything but seriously negative reasons.

Archie still had a couple of scars that were testament to that. But they'd been drawn together. Now they were on the same side, linked together and fighting for the same thing. If I wavered in my determination, their faith would push me through.

"Then I better go get the others ready. Bentham, if you would be so kind?" Archie requested.

She nodded and reached into her pocket to pull out Thrash's portal key.

"Thank you, Bentham," I added.

She smiled. "Don't thank me yet. Wait until we make it through, and you don't end up in The Deep. We don't have the best track record of using this thing yet."

I laughed. "Noted. And if we fail, there's a good chance you'll be sharing The Deep with me." She gave one more smile, let out a resolute breath, and disappeared. I waited for a few seconds while staring into the empty spot where she had stood. "All right. Let's do this thing."

I let memory guide me as I walked toward my fate.

CHAPTER THIRTY-THREE

As much as I appreciated having Dog and Archie with me, there was a sense of peace in the solitude as I walked along the sidewalk alone. It was eerie following this path again. I had scattered, fragmented memories of walking it so long before, when I was a little girl.

So much had changed around me, yet it was still the same. That was what I wanted. I knew what was ahead of me, and the comfort and reassurance gave me strength.

When I reached St. Michael's Church, some of that slipped away. The last time I was here was the day we said our final goodbyes to my mother. As far as I knew, none of us had been here after that. Death entered my life for the first time that day, and it hadn't made itself a stranger since. Hopefully, the Reaper Man wasn't coming for me this time.

But if he was, at least it was in the same place where my mother had gone to whatever was beyond. Maybe she could put in a good word for me.

When I opened the door and stepped inside, the smell

washed over me. It was clean and soft, old like dried paper and deeply polished wood. It was a smell I would never forget. I walked into the chapel and sat in the same pew I occupied years before. This was where I listened to the sermon. It was where I cried through my mother's funeral. It was the last time I ever sat inside a holy place.

Sitting there in the space that seemed to remember me as much as I remembered it, I thought about all the things I'd been through over the last ten years. It was a strange place to be. It was firmly my story, with all the horrific pain and grotesque smells and sights burned into my memory to prove it, but it also felt like a movie I'd seen. It was difficult to wrap my head around the concept that all of it had been real as I sat there in the dark, quiet church.

I could almost convince myself it was only my imagination—that I didn't get dragged through a hole in the fabric of reality and brought to another realm. That I didn't lose ten years of my life to the filthy brutality of an otherworldly prison.

At the same time, that experience defined me. More than anything else in my life, it made me who I was, and there was no going back from that. Nothing would ever change it. All I could do was use what I went through to do what needed doing. This ended now.

I'd been sitting in the church for almost half an hour when I heard the door open behind me. There was no need to turn around and look. I knew who it was. I took one more moment to brace myself and find strength in my surroundings and my confidence in myself then rose from the pew. I stood in the middle of the aisle and turned to look at the chapel door.

Rand stood alone in the doorway, her robes hanging long and her eyes glaring at me so intensely that I felt them, although the darkness in the building veiled her expression.

"A church?" she sneered. " Why would you want to meet me here?"

I looked around again as she arrogantly swaggered toward me.

"I came to this church for a reason. It's beautiful, and much like me, has seen a lot. Besides, the oldest church in the city seemed like the perfect place to fight the devil."

With that, Rand attacked.

She surprised me with her speed as she leapt through the air with a gracefulness that would have been awe-inspiring if it wasn't outright terrifying, and thrust-kicked me in my jaw. I stumbled backward and sprawled out by the pulpit.

The kick had landed hard, and I was a little dizzy as I regained my feet, but I had gone with the momentum enough that I wasn't too badly hurt. Which was a good thing, since she was nearly on top of me already. I threw an elbow into her stomach to stop her forward motion.

She bent over with surprise at the blow, and I quickly raised my knee to smash into her face. She saw it coming, though, and caught my leg, then swept the other one and forced me back down onto the floor. I rolled out of the way in time to avoid her fist and scrambled to my feet.

I spun to face her, but she was already there, impossibly fast and powerful as she smashed my nose with her fist. I backed up, but she hit me again in the jaw, then landed a third strike to my stomach. It was enough to open me up, and she kicked me in the ribs.

I went down again and crawled away. I had to create some space to form a plan. She was so damned fast, and every hit was like being smashed with a bowling ball. Cyclopes hit softer than she did. It was insane. I crawled onto the stage and behind the pulpit, and Rand followed me.

I was ready for her when she came around the pulpit and threw the communion plate at her like a religious frisbee. It dinged her in the head. It was enough to distract her. I leapt up and tackled her off the stage, and we crashed through a table. Fliers for the church's Sunday Brunch and sign-ups for the recreational sports teams flew through the air as I struggled to get to my knees.

Before I could get up, a hard kick landed in my stomach. It was like someone had smashed me with a sledgehammer, and all the wind flew out of me in a hard, tight wheeze. I rolled to my side away from her and toward the pews while coughing. Blood trickled from my mouth, and I was reasonably sure I was bleeding internally.

Rand stood where she had kicked me and half-laughed, then pushed the pew closest to her away with ease. It flew off to the side and crashed into a wall. I made a note to hit her extra hard for wrecking the church and doubled it when she tossed another pew on the opposite side. She was toying with me by clearing a space for me to run and attack her, knowing that she had the upper hand. I tried to breathe deep as I let myself sit with the pain in my stomach and ribs and acknowledged my new normal of feeling like I had a hole knocked through me.

I reached up and grabbed the nearest pew, then clawed my way across the aisle and dragged myself up to sit.

"I suppose I don't need to tell you I got your message," Rand commented with a sarcastic bite in her voice.

I wrapped one arm around my stomach to hold in the intestines that felt like they would tumble out at any second and smiled. The pain didn't matter. This was why we were here. Rand getting my message meant Bentham succeeded in her part of the plan.

That was one step down.

"I figured threatening to reveal the truth about you and your past would get you here." I coughed. Rand gritted her teeth angrily, but I kept going. "If anyone knew what you really are, they'd hate you. You spent your entire adult life trying to build up this image of yourself. The most powerful Philosopher among all of The Far. The greatest and the strongest, the most influential. Only, nobody realized you were crafting a story to cover up what you are and where you came from. You couldn't stand the possibility of them finding out you're half-human. It would disgust them."

She took a threatening step toward me. "How did you learn about me?"

"My mother's old scrapbook. You thought you were clever when you mentioned her, didn't you? Thought you could throw her memory in my face to hurt me, but I'd never figure out anything else. It was all part of your arrogance, your delusion that no one could best you. Only, you didn't take into account who you messed with. Me. It was your first big mistake. I found her scrapbook and went through it until I found a picture of her fifteenth birthday party. You remember that day, don't you? There in your little hat, separated from everybody else. So strange and out of place."

"Shut up." Her voice climbed as she grew angrier.

My strength somewhat returned, I pulled myself up off the pew and stepped into the aisle.

"Figuring out you were raised in the human world was easy. Learning the truth about your father was the hard part. Although, honestly, I should have known. It even flickered through my mind once how much you sounded like him. When I read your manifesto, I couldn't help thinking that it had his cadence."

"Don't you fucking say anything like that again," Rand spat. "Solon wasn't my father. He was a piece of shit and a traitor to his people."

"Now, now, Ayn. You really shouldn't say things like that about your dad. Especially not here in the church. Honor thy mother and thy father, you know. It's one of the big ones—part of the Big Guy's Manifesto. Of course, his has more staying power than yours. You should show more respect to your father."

My baiting finally worked. I could almost hear the precise moment when Rand snapped.

"He never deserved my respect. He destroyed my life. I was only ten years old when he abandoned me on Earth by getting arrested for breaking the *Pax Philosophia*. Living among humans was horrible. It was pure torment for the next six years. I was better than them in every way, yet they mocked me.

"They excluded me and ensured I was the butt of every joke. It disgusted me that I couldn't do anything about it. I knew who and what I was. Yet there was nothing I could do against these grotesque, flimsy little humans who dared treat me that way. I couldn't use my magic against them or do anything that would prove how fragile and meaningless they were.

"Like your mother. She died before I could get my vengeance on her, so I did the next best thing. I framed your father. Or at least, I tried to. Having her eldest child take the blame was an acceptable consolation."

I steeled myself against the moment. She was trying to bait me into making the first move by plucking at my buttons. She wanted me to fly into a rage and make a mistake.

"So that's why you want to end the *Pax*? Because of the way the humans treated you?" I needled as I continued to lure her deeper into the murk and chaos of her mind.

"That isn't the only reason. Humans are weak. Their existence is futile. Yet it's the Philosophers who lose their right to their natural gifts and abilities. I want to destroy the *Pax* because it holds Philosophers back from doing what they want," Rand snarled.

"And other Farsiders, too. Right? They should be able to live their lives freely and do whatever they want, even on Earth?" I baited.

"I don't give a shit about the other Farsiders," Rand raged. "They're only tools. Weapons. My minions are working on the final stroke. They're cracking open The Deep to unleash its hell upon your puny world. I will force humans to confront what lurks in their darkest night-mares. When the humans kill those monsters, it will galvanize the rest of The Far into fighting back, with me at the helm."

She grinned, an evil, maniacal expression, and I felt bile rise in my throat in sheer disgust of her. I knew what hell she planned to unleash, better than almost anyone else in the universe. I had lived it and survived it. The rest of the world wouldn't be so lucky.

"Millions will die, Near and Far alike," I pointed out.

"Who the hell cares? In the end, they'll crown me as ruler of the whole pile of ash."

I shook my head. "That's not going to happen."

"Why?"

"They won't be able to collect enough pieces of you to put back together for the crown to fit."

Rand lunged at me. She didn't realize that the entire time we'd talked, I'd guided her down the aisle and toward the chapel's side door. When she flew at me, I grabbed her and braced myself for impact.

We smashed through the door and landed in a heap on the floor right at Senator Cabot's feet. A bunch of wide-eyed reporters with television monitors surrounded her. To the other side was Bentham, flanked by several members of the Guild.

Rand stood and looked at them all in disbelief. Her mouth opened and shut like a trout in the deep sea. She turned wild-eyed toward me, then back to them. Her plan was shot, and she had lost.

They had heard the whole thing.

CHAPTER THIRTY-FOUR

Rand bellowed in rage and slammed her fist into the floor. The room shook, and the boards split, creating a deep crater that shot like an arrow toward the cameras. Everyone dove to safety and Rand smashed her other hand into the ground below, which set off an explosion along the fault line.

I saw her shadow pass me in the smoke and fire as she ran for the door to escape. I scrambled to my feet, and my eyes fell on Senator Cabot and the various reporters struggling to rise. They seemed to have escaped the worst. Bentham was already on her feet, and our eyes met.

"Make sure everyone is okay. I'll go after her," I shouted. I dove through a line of scorching flame that singed the bottom of my hair. Behind me, I heard the Guild members muttering to each other. They would follow me soon. The plan had worked.

I tore through the door and out onto the street. Rand was ahead of me and ducking away around a corner, headed toward the Battery. The crowd that usually hovered around the landmark seawall was always full of school children on Civil War history field trips and history buffs.

I needed to get there before she did. I tried to catch up, but she was too fast as she ducked around a building and into the bright sunlight of the day. There were hundreds of people around. Rand would have counted on it.

We were only blocks away. I could hear the buzz of the crowd waiting there. Rand was ahead of me, but barely, and was tossing anything she passed in my way so I had to jump over or go around it. She was trying to get someplace where she felt like she had the upper hand. Somewhere with allies.

Boy, was she in for a surprise.

When she rounded a large Victorian house that had stood on the shore of Charleston through hurricanes, war, and plague, Rand came face-to-face with the building's latest historic moment. She had planned it this way herself. This was the scene of her invasion, her grand plan to unleash hell upon the world.

But something was wrong. I could see it in her eyes— she knew. The portal stood where she had planned, between two large cannons at the edge of the courtyard. It was the perfect metaphorical place to fire the first shot.

And it was live. It glowed white and green as it buzzed with electricity and energy and magic, but an army surrounded it. Enemies stood there instead of hundreds of civilians waiting like lambs for the slaughter. I stopped as she skidded to a halt, looked in each direction, and realized she was surrounded.

The Vrya stood in front of the portal, along with the West Virginian miners and townsfolk who had joined them. Some faced Rand, but most faced the gate, ready and waiting. To the north stood Pip and the Lizard People who flanked her in grim-eyed determination as their chests rose in deep but quickening breaths.

They were ready for battle. A mixture of humans and Farsiders occupied the south—Far and Near allies who Rand had tricked and turned against one another. Now they watched her with hatred in their eyes. She turned back to the west, to me. Archie calmly walked up behind me, close enough that I could hear his voice when he half-whispered to me.

"The Deep will pour through any second now. We couldn't stop it. But we're ready. You keep your focus on her. Let your allies have your back."

I nodded and took a few steps closer to Rand. She was still spinning in each direction, unsure of what to do. Her hand was locked in an open position, and it sparked with magic.

"How…" she began, "why?"

"You were fighting for a failed system," I began, keeping my voice level and even despite the adrenaline coursing through my veins. "But you were right about one thing. The *Pax* is terrible. For both The Near and The Far. It keeps everyone in darkness, separated, cold, and distant. Instead of coming together and flourishing, it keeps us apart and at each other's throats."

"Bullshit," Rand spat. "Bullshit!" she screamed to the crowd at large, then turned back to me. "It won't work. It will never work. The Near and The Far cannot coexist."

"Maybe." I stepped closer again. I was within feet of her now. "Maybe we can't. Maybe we'll tear each other apart in a war that will devastate us both. Maybe you'll get your wish, and we'll be kingdoms of ash. Or..."

I stepped close enough that I could reach her now. My eyes locked on hers. They pulsed in her skull, and the veins seemed to glow bright red. Sweat rolled down her face and fell into the curve of her mouth and onto her lips. "Perhaps we don't go to war. Perhaps without the fearsome Hobbes instigating hatred, we have a chance. Maybe the only Farsider who can't live in peace with The Near is you. And, ironically, the only Nearsider who can't live in peace with The Far is...you."

"I'll kill you all myself if I have to," she screamed, her voice shrill and piercing. Her attack followed. She threw a blast of magic at me, and I dodged enough that it only caught my shoulder and knocked me back and onto the ground, but didn't hurt me. Several of the Vrya stepped forward, but I held my hand up to them. Rand was mine.

She reached into her belt for something as I stood. When I got to my feet, she pulled out a small metal block with a button on it. She pressed the button and spun to the portal, her eyes wide and crazed. A giggle of madness bubbled up from her chest.

"I'll do it myself," she screeched, "but I won't have to!"

The portal pulsed and creatures from The Deep poured out. The Vrya and the miners were ready. Pip and the lizards flanked them and held the line while the Farsiders and humans from the south made the resistance even deeper.

"Flank left, my scaly friends," Pip cried, and they moved as one, their wide eyes rolling in their terrified yet resolute faces. Everything I had heard about them was that they were easily spooked and avoided confrontation. However, as the Harbingers approached, they looked far more imposing. "Attack!"

As creatures came through, they were lifted off their feet, pulled to the side, and beaten until they were incapacitated. The army of the resistance moved like one, with Archie and Pip shouting orders from behind.

"No, you don't need to eat their faces," Pip exclaimed, and I turned back to Rand, a grin I couldn't stop stretching from one ear to the other.

Rand's face became a mask of horror. She was witnessing her plan destroyed. I relished the thought that she was losing, and there was nothing she could do. She could only watch. She slowly turned toward me, her jaw set open and her nostrils wide as she breathed heavily in anger.

"You," she growled, "were supposed to die!"

She lunged, and I moved barely in time. She crumpled to the ground, and I kicked her in the ribs. I heard the crunch, but she shrugged it off, grasped my foot while it was in contact with her, and turned me so I fell on my face. I rolled to my back and kicked her off. She had tried to twist my ankle, to break it quickly before I could get her off me. It was a tactic I recognized.

It was something Solon taught me a long time ago.

Like lesson after lesson in The Deep, she attacked her downed opponent from the legs. Incapacitation was the key. If you could stop the enemy from moving, you could stop them from fighting. Her fingers reached for my legs, but I rolled backward over my head and away from her. I stood and took off toward her in a direct line.

She would expect it, and I knew that, but I had to make her think it. Fighting was more about what your opponent thinks you're going to do than what you do. Solon had said that, too. Over and over. If she thought I was coming head-on, she would react like it.

Sure enough, she went low right before I reached her, aiming to tackle my legs preemptively. Instead, I leapt up, somersaulted over her, and landed on my feet behind her. She was on her knees after she missed my legs, and I spun to plant my knee in the side of her head. She hit the ground hard but swung a fist up as I leapt onto her. It caught me in the cheek and crackled with energy that sent shockwaves down my spine and made me roll off her.

She was smart. I went high instead of low once, and it worked, but it wouldn't again. I rolled to the side and jumped up. She was on her feet also, but dizzy. I had a shot, and I needed to take it.

I reached behind me and grabbed the amulet, kept safe in a pocket on my belt. I yanked it out and pressed my thumb in its center, then heard a vacuum-like sound. Energy flooded my veins. Suddenly, I felt like I could move mountains, my bruises didn't hurt so bad, and the world around me seemed slower than I was. The amulet was at full strength, and now, so was I.

Rand was on her feet, one arm pulled behind her. It had begun to glow black, a magical blast that assuredly carried the ability to kill. I ran directly for her, then crouched low to gain as much momentum as possible. I held the amulet in one hand and the other I balled into a fist.

My foot pressed hard into the ground to gain as much force as possible. I punched up as I leapt into the uppercut like I was trying to get the height to dunk a basketball. There was a rush of sound and the crack of Rand's jaw under my fist.

She rose several feet into the air and flew until she slammed to the ground, and her hand fizzled out. She was disoriented, but not knocked out. My hand hurt like hell, and I was sure I broke it, but it didn't matter. I rushed toward her, expecting to be able to finish her easily now. Instead, she moved quickly and unexpectedly and kicked my legs out from under me.

I tumbled to my back and rolled, barely dodging a black and purple haze of a fist that crashed into the ground beside me and sent dirt and grass into the air. I kicked at her and landed a vicious knee smash. She crumpled. I leapt up and drew my fist back to pound her jaw. She pulled hers back and caught me as I fell toward her.

The lights went out for a moment, and I was dimly aware of my arm being pinned awkwardly behind me as I hit the ground. My shoulder strained in the odd position. As I tried to get my bearings, Rand appeared in my vision, the sun shining high behind her in a cloudless sky.

"The same person may have trained us, but I'm better," she gloated. The amulet coursed new energy through me. My shoulder didn't hurt anymore, and I felt the adrenaline pumping through me.

I smiled.

"Solon gave you a lot. And you rejected it. He loved you. But he loved me too. And he gave awesome gifts."

I pulled out the amulet and let it catch the sunlight. Rand's face fell as she recognized it, and she stepped back. I hopped to my feet as if I were weightless and charged.

She put her hands up to block, but I punched right through them, crashing into her jaw and her ribs, and heard them crack beneath my fist. I spun and landed a roundhouse kick to her chest, and she spiraled backward onto the ground.

I reached into my pocket and pulled the only weapon I could trust—the only one I needed.

The switchblade.

I ran toward her, my voice filling the air with a roar of triumph and expectation. Rand was on her feet but facing away. She turned to see me, and her hand glowed black again. Before she could throw it at me, I lunged. The knife ran her through in the stomach, and we crumpled to the ground together.

Our faces were inches apart. She looked down to see the blood pouring from her, covering my hand and the handle of the knife. She looked back up into my face, and calmness settled over her.

"Finish me." A smile cracked the edges of her lips.

Right then, I hated her more than I ever had. She thought she won. She thought she was free and that the war would continue in her absence. She was wrong.

"No." I grabbed the knife and pulled it out of her. She lurched when I did. I quickly spun it and slammed it down across her hand, slicing it off completely.

She screamed in horror and pain as I stood. "I won't kill

you, but I will leave you without your magic. Without your hand, you're powerless. And now..." I turned to see the open portal, the resistance flanking it, and monsters of The Deep in various states of life and consciousness on the ground. "The Deep is empty. I can't imagine a better person to be the first new resident than you."

CHAPTER THIRTY-FIVE

"A girl walks into a bar wearing rags with an unidentified rodent in her jacket pocket. The bartender says they don't have any tacos but brings her a slice of pizza."

The man behind the bar looked at me quizzically.

"I don't get it. Where's the joke?" he asked.

"There is no joke. That's the night I escaped from prison," I told him. "The bartender was you. I wanted to know if you recognized the story and remembered me."

That changed the look from quizzical to confused, and he turned away to see to a sudden cocktail-related emergency on the other side of the bar. That was just as well. Several of the multiple TVs set up around the bar were showing the news, and I was interested in watching.

That's not something I ever would have thought I would say when I was spending an evening in a bar. Of course, I never got to the point in my regular human life when I would have been bar-hopping and learning the intricate ways of socializing among the liquor-soaked and tobacco-stained. That was much more Ally's area of expertise.

If I had followed in her footsteps and made it out to the bars, however, I honestly didn't think I would be clamoring to watch the news broadcast. Not that I could imagine many bars frequently had the news splashed on the majority of their screens. From what I understood, they usually reserved them for far more riveting entertainment, like sports.

But that night, the bar was fascinated by the same stories unfolding in the news that had caught the attention of what I could imagine was virtually everyone else in existence. As I stared at the screen, a reporter held out her microphone, and the camera's focus pulled back to reveal a goblin standing beside her.

"Yes, it's true," the goblin said with a convincing nod. "We've been around all this time. Humans simply haven't noticed us."

"And how does that make you feel?" the reporter asked. "To live in a world where you're ignored and not noticed by the other beings around you?"

The goblin looked at her strangely, like she didn't fully comprehend the question.

"It was intentional," she replied.

The reporter pulled the microphone back to her mouth while shaking her head and staring meaningfully into the camera.

"You heard it right here. Intentional invisibility. Feeling so lost in a world that wasn't their own that they felt they were purposely erased. That's heartbreaking to hear. I don't know about you, viewers, but this reporter is looking forward to finding ways to make amends and welcome tolerance and friendship among our neighbors. Back to you, Tom."

The image on the screen changed to inside a broad-casting studio. A tall man in a blue suit and bold, square black glasses shook his head.

"There's so much for us to learn," he said.

I scoffed. It was a fun new pastime listening to interviews and news stories and seeing how much the humans were managing to misinterpret what the Farsiders said. I guessed I couldn't blame them. All this was utterly new to them, and they weren't yet used to seeing all the different types of creatures roaming around the streets and existing in the same spaces they were.

I suppose they weren't used to them existing in any other spaces, either. I still had to remind myself sometimes that most humans didn't know anything about The Far and the creatures that originated there. They couldn't help not knowing what to think about them and to essentially flail around trying to figure out what was going on and how these creatures might think.

That was an interesting tendency of humans. Always wanting to figure out what others were thinking, but rarely getting it right. That was evident from all the different newscasts blaring around me on the various screens. Each channel seemed to have their skewed way to look at the war, and everything that had happened since Rand and the Harbingers stormed Earth.

Interviews were happening with all sorts of Farsiders and humans, getting their perspectives and recording their recollections. Some of the news channels made the entire situation seem incredibly bad and tense. There were more than a few shocked and appalled humans, and fights periodically broke out. But that was to be expected. Yet another growing pain of a society trying to figure out the virtual explosion of what they all thought was reality.

On the other hand, a lot of channels were shining a far more positive light on the situation. They saw an opportunity for growth and learning, to broaden our horizons and learn to coexist, although some of the motivation was fear of what Farsiders might be capable of.

"Hey." The bartender stepped in front of me again. "So, you said you came in here the night you escaped from prison. Do you mean that messed-up prison where all the monsters came from?"

"The Deep?" I didn't take my eyes off the interview happening on the screen in front of me. "Yep, I do."

An interviewer had approached a cluster of fairies and was asking a series of interesting, in-depth questions. He wasn't trying to interpret what they were saying or sensationalize. It was good to see him taking a genuine interest in them so he could educate the humans watching although it did give me a case of the twitches while remembering my less-than-pleasant run-ins with the fairies.

"Holy shit," the bartender exclaimed. "So that was you who fought that giant dude and dragged him out of the bar, right?"

"Troll," I told him. "About to eat the woman he was hitting on. Don't worry. The Far officers got him before he could snack on anybody. Or drown."

I remembered what the monstrous creature looked like

face-down in the puddle, and couldn't help but crack a small smile.

"And the unidentified rodent? Was that some kind of prison code? Far slang or something?"

Still not taking my eyes off the screen, I rummaged in the pocket of my leather jacket and pulled out Splinter. I held him up by the scruff of his neck in front of the bartender's face. Out of the corner of my eye, I saw his little hands clutching a pretzel I'd smuggled down to him as he happily munched away. The bartender made a choking sound somewhere in his throat and rushed away again. I looked at Splinter.

"Don't listen to him. You're still the cutest toilet brush gliding rat who has ever been."

I kissed him and stuffed him back in my pocket. One of my fingers went through a hole in the leather, and I looked down at the jacket. It was scuffed, torn, ripped, and stained with a variety of substances I didn't much care to dwell on.

Maybe it was time to retire it. At least tonight's return to the bar where I stole it from a drunk man was a touching send-off.

"...did you call me Tinkerbell?" the voice on the screen said in a high pitch right before a load of other voices interjected, and the reporter threw it back to the studio in a hurry.

"Is that Pip?" someone behind me asked.

I looked over my shoulder to see Bentham coming toward me. She was looking at the screen to my side. I glanced at it, laughed, and nodded.

"Yep. That would be Pip. She's been doing the interview

circuits for the last few days. She's quite the internet sensation now," I told the Philosopher.

"Sounds about right. I bet she loves that."

"Pip was born for greatness."

Bentham smiled and sat on the barstool beside me. Her eyes fell on the empty glass in front of me. "No second round?"

"I would, but the bartender is afraid of me."

"Ah. Well, it happens." She drew a breath. "So, I have some news."

"What's up?" I turned to face her.

"I have been unanimously elected as a representative of the Guild. The Chief of Near/Far Relations," she announced and smiled happily.

"That's fantastic. Congratulations. You'll be amazing at that."

"Yes, but it's a big job. I mean, nobody knows what the hell is going on right now. We find groups of mixed humans and Farsiders, and we don't know if they're going to hold hands and sing Kumbaya, or if they'll start chasing each other with pointy sticks and molten sugar."

I tilted my head at her. "Did you get that from Archie?"

"I did. Why?"

"He saw *Troop Beverly Hills* recently, and I don't think he quite caught on to the idea of a s'more." I closed my eyes and shook my head, then waved my hand in front of me to brush the thought away. "Never mind. It doesn't matter. Go on."

"What I was saying is, it's a big job. I could use your help."

I let out a long breath. "I'm done being famous for a while. I simply want life to go back to normal."

Bentham laughed. "Normal is dead."

"Then a new normal."

She got down off her stool. "Well, think about it. Let me know later. I'm off to sign peace agreements with Senator Cabot. My first official duty."

I smiled and waved at her. "Have fun."

"One more thing." She turned back and reached into her pocket. For a brief second, all the times of running from Bentham flashed before my eyes, and despite myself, my instincts immediately went into preparation for fight mode.

But instead of pulling out a weapon or her lasso or some electric cuffs or something, she simply pulled out a folded white sheet of paper. She held it out to me and smiled. I took it and eyed her suspiciously as my adrenaline drained.

"What's this?" I unfolded the paper.

"A full pardon for Sara Slickerman. You're officially a free woman now. I couldn't ask you to help if you were still technically on our Most Wanted list."

I didn't know how to respond. A smile stretched across my face, and a tear threatened to drop from one of my eyes, but I sniffed it back. Instead, I opted for the nuclear option. I reached out and wrapped her in a hug.

"Oh, whoa. Okay. Very nice. You're very welcome." She patted me on the back with the practiced cadence of someone who has never expressed anything even remotely close to physical displays of friendship. "I have to go now," she mumbled, and I let her go. As she turned, I saw the faint hint of a smile on her face.

She left, and I turned back to watch the last of Pip's most recent interviews while draining the last drops of the beer in front of me and smiling fondly at her animated retelling of the battle.

"Barkeep!" I shouted. "Stop hiding behind the vodka sign and give me another round." I grinned. "I'm a free woman!"

CHAPTER THIRTY-SIX

After Bentham left, I disappeared back into watching more of the news, and staring in awe at a world completely changed. I didn't know what I expected when I thought about what would happen after destroying Hobbes by revealing the existence of The Far to the humans. I knew it was the only option.

That was the only way I could bring her down and protect the world. In the beginning, I thought keeping them in the dark and maintaining the separation between the two realms was critical to keeping Earth and its inhabitants safe. But then I realized that wasn't the case.

It took finding out about Rand and learning the truth about Solon for me to piece it all together. Her entire life was a lie. She was immensely powerful. There was nothing that could hide that. But the only reason she had that incredible degree of power and magical ability was because of her father.

My mentor, my dear friend, was not only a good man but an exceptional Philosopher. He was different than the others and saw the world in a way that many believed was wrong. I saw it as progressive and encouraging. Although he had to give his life for it, Solon ushered in a new time.

Somehow, he knew I would figure it out. He knew one day I would learn the truth about his daughter and the secrets she kept. Those secrets nearly destroyed everything. And that's how I knew continuing to hide The Far would never work. As massive and potentially disastrous as it was, we had to blow the lid off it and let everybody know what was going on.

Once the truth was out, Hobbes didn't have leverage anymore. There was still a war fought between the realms, but it was nowhere near as massive in scale or as deadly an effect as she planned.

I went into my plan of revealing The Far with the sole intention of protecting lives both Near and Far. I didn't let myself think beyond that, to what the world would be like when we revealed the realms, and all the species were mixed. It could have been unimaginably horrific.

The humans could have aggressively rejected the concept of The Far creatures existing among them. The Farsiders could have decided they were tired of hiding and wanted to gain dominance over the humans and take over the Earth altogether. But that wasn't what happened. Of course, there was some animosity. There were conflicts and tension. People didn't understand on both sides. In some ways, those feelings would likely always exist to some degree. All we could hope was that there would be more tolerance and acceptance than there was resistance.

"Taco Tuesday."

The words cut through my contemplation, and I looked

up at the bartender. He had gathered the courage to approach me again, but stood a couple of feet back and held a plate.

"Excuse me?"

"I remembered what you said when you were first here. You asked for tacos and mentioned Taco Tuesday. I told you we had tacos on Fridays."

"Because of Tortellini Tuesday," I recalled and nodded.

"Yes. Well, we changed it. Now it's Fettucini Fridays. Made more sense."

"Wait," I blurted out far more loudly than I intended, "what is today? Is it Friday?" I realized I'd completely lost track of the days despite all the news I'd absorbed.

"No, Tuesday."

"Then does that mean…" The anticipation nearly killed me.

"That's right." The bartender nodded and shoved the plate toward me. "Tofu Tuesday."

I blinked.

"To…fu? Tuesday?"

"Yeah, so it matches. Like you said." He grinned.

I looked down at the admittedly decent-looking plate of tofu nuggets. He had gone through the effort of making them look like little smiley faces. I feigned a smile.

"Thanks," I choked out, trying not to sound bitter and disappointed.

"Oh, and," he pulled a napkin out of his pocket. "I didn't think he'd mind, considering… Just considering."

I took the folded napkin from him and unfolded it in my hand to reveal a tiny plate, no bigger than the palm of my hand, piled high with tofu nuggets.

"Thank you. Splinter, look at what he has for you." Splinter's little head popped out of my pocket, and I lowered the plate toward him. He eagerly snatched it and buried himself back in my pocket. "Say thank you."

He instantly scrambled out and leapt toward the bartender, then ran up his arm and rubbed his face against the man's cheek before he could scuttle away.

"Oh. Wow," the bartender said.

It was clear to anyone looking at him that he would rather peel off his skin and learn to live as a skeleton than stand there bonding with Splinter, but he managed to stay calm until my little guy rushed back to his pocket.

"Good boy." I looked at the bartender. "That was sweet."

He nodded, the expression on his face somewhere between terrified and proud of himself for being so woke and walked away, leaving me to tofu nuggets. They weren't as good as street tacos, but in the grander scheme of life, they were warm and chewy, and the dip he made for them was extra tangy and sweet at the same time.

Not to mention that I was grateful I still had teeth to chew them and a stomach located in its proper inner-body position to digest it. Loss of one or both were definite possibilities not too long before.

When I finished eating, I was ready to leave. I walked out of the bar and a piercingly bright blast of light in my eyes briefly blinded me. When my vision came back, I saw Dog standing in front of me.

"Seriously? After all this, you're still popping up out of nowhere and catching me off-guard?"

"You don't need to be on guard. That's what I do," he smoothly returned.

He fell into step beside me as we leisurely walked down the sidewalk. Neither of us said anything for a while. Frankly, I was unsure of what to say at all. This was uncharted territory for me. Before getting yanked out of reality, I had little to no experience with guys.

A few awkward dates. Middle school dances that never turned out the way the girls dreamed. I was more focused on school, friends, and helping take care of my sisters than I was the dating scene. Then life dragged my ass and threw me off every path I ever imagined myself being on.

Going through a wildly different meaning of arrested development wasn't exactly where I envisioned any kind of romantic feelings developing. Yet, here I was, crushing on Dog. Entertaining such silly yet wonderful thoughts as wishing he would reach over and hold my hand. Every little girl who presided over their wedding to their favorite stuffed animal, eat your heart out.

This was so strange and exciting and disquieting and thrilling and everything all at the same time. I didn't know what to think or say or do. At that moment, I barely knew if I was walking correctly since I seemed to have lost all spatial awareness of my body and felt completely out of control of it.

Finally, it felt like we'd been walking for hours in silence and I decided to say something. But before I could, Dog jumped in.

"Listen, the last time I went on a date was during the harvest moon in 2017, and it didn't go so well. But I was wondering..."

I felt his discomfort and interjected, "I haven't been on a

date since a week after I got my braces off. I think there's enough awkwardness to go around."

Dog grinned. "How about next Tuesday?"

I nodded and turned to him so I could gather him in a hug.

"Thank you," I whispered against the side of his neck, then released him. "I need to run and meet up with the others. Want to come?"

He shook his head. "No, I have some important dog things to do. Mailmen to chase, cars to bark at, that sort of thing." He smiled at his little joke, and I laughed. "Go on, get going."

I smiled and rushed off, feeling a spark of happiness I hadn't felt in a long time.

CHAPTER THIRTY-SEVEN

After the horror of the battle with the released monsters from The Deep, I thought I would never want to see the Battery again. But I couldn't stay away from it. This was home. It was the place I loved and had longed for during every one of those miserable days I spent in The Deep. I couldn't let anything take the joy of being back here away from me. Being free and able to simply sit on a bench and look at the ocean.

So, that's what we were doing. Archie and Ally sandwiched me as I stared out over the water, and watched the sunlight dance on the tips of the ripples flowing to and from the land. I thought I would never want to see this place again, but I was wrong. Now that I was here, it felt like I could never leave and would be happy staring at the water for eternity.

Everything seemed perfect as we sat there. Or, at least, as close as I could imagine it to be. My mind was too scarred to truly believe anything was perfect ever again, but I was all right with that. It meant I could still discover new and wonderful things. Not finding perfection meant I hadn't reached my peak and never would. There would always be more to see, more to strive for.

But this moment on the bench in Charleston with my heart still humming about Dog asking me out was as close as I needed to be. The sun was out, glowing around us and reflecting off the water.

The sea was calm and added a hint of salty scent and cool touch to the breeze that came up off it and broke the warm air. We sat there staring at it together, hovering in the moment in time. I didn't want to speak and ruin it, to shatter the beautiful, peaceful serenity.

"So, what in the living hell happened?"

Thank you, Ally. Moment over.

I glanced over at her. "What?"

"Seriously. What happened? I mean, I was there. I know what happened, but I can't believe it."

"Neither can I," Archie agreed. "That was…" he paused and shook his head, then let a breath stream out from between his lips. "That was a lot. Even for me, and I deal in some pretty shady stuff."

"I can't believe it, either. And I'm the messed-up one who came up with it. Now that it's all over and both of you are alive and still in possession of all your limbs, I can tell you that there were some touch-and-go moments when I didn't know if everything would work out. Actually, there were a lot of moments when I didn't know. There were full swathes of time I was pretty sure my head was about ten minutes out from being turned into a tetherball for The

Deep's recreation room, with my entrails playing the role of string."

"But here you are. Fully intact," Ally noted.

"And very glad about it."

"Oh, come on," Archie protested. "You're being modest. Everybody knows what a badass you are. You're the infamous Sara Slick. Slayer of angels and kicker-in-the-shins of vampires."

I laughed. "Well, Arch, I guess you're out of work now that everything has changed. What will you do with yourself? Revive the mobile lab and roam the country doing science demonstrations for birthday parties?"

"What are you talking about?"

"After all this, you won't have anything to do. The rune market will go straight to shit," I pointed out.

Archie laughed. "Are you kidding me? Now that we've blown everything wide open, there are a ton of Nearsiders who will want to get their hands on my wares. My phone has been blowing up with offers for work. Everybody wants to get a little taste of magic now."

"What do you mean, offers for work? Don't tell me Charleston is going to turn into a hub for black market Farstuff."

"Wasn't it already? I seem to remember that's kind of what got us into all this in the first place."

"I can vouch for that," Ally agreed. "Archie seemed pretty at home in that warehouse when we first found him."

Archie laughed, then shook his head. "I won't be in Charleston."

That took the life right out of me. Ally, too.

"You won't?" she asked.

"I'm going to take a gig out of Tucson. It'll be a great opportunity to get a change of pace. Some new surroundings," he told us.

"That sounds great. I'm happy for you."

"Then why don't you look like it?"

"I'm also a little sad," I admitted. "Everything has finally worked out, and we can kind of be, without that annoying constant threat of death and destruction, and now you'll be gone."

"Yeah." He gave us a brief sad look followed by a smile. "But you know where to find me. If you need me, I'll be there. And I'll find my way back. Tucson isn't forever. I don't do well in the dry heat."

I laughed. "Neither do your goldfish, so make sure to bring their full three ounces of water."

"What about you, Ally? What will you do now that it's over?" He leaned forward so he could look across me to her.

That glimmer was still there between them, the hint of a spark buried beneath some tension and a whole lot of awkward. I had a feeling Archie was right about Tucson. It wouldn't be forever.

"I've decided it's time to connect with my roots."

"Oh, lord." I rolled my eyes. "Alejandra is making her return. What are you going to do? Become a tequila distiller? Open a restaurant? Weave sarapes?"

She glared at me. "Again, Slick. Offensive. And inaccurate. Even for you."

"I know." I grinned. "I was trying to come up with a couple more stereotypes for the wrong cultures, but couldn't think of any."

"Thank goodness for that." She looked at Archie again. "I'm going to settle down in PR and finally do some serious writing."

"About donkeys and windmills!" I shouted. They glared at me. "Don Quixote? No?"

She looked at Archie again.

"Are you going to do investigative reporting?" he asked.

"No. It's more like historical fiction."

"Oh? What's it called?"

Ally and I exchanged glances and smiled.

"The Heinous Crimes of Sara Slickerman."

She made me laugh.

"Slickerman?" Archie asked, and I laughed even harder.

"You know, I think you're onto something, Alejandra. You aren't the only one who needs to connect to her roots," I admitted.

"I should get going," Archie noted. "They're expecting me in Tucson tomorrow."

He gathered me in a hug and said goodbye, then moved over to Ally. They looked at each other uncomfortably for a few seconds before hugging. It was an odd experience, watching two people who wanted to hug each other struggle so hard to seem like they didn't. They exchanged goodbyes, then Archie turned to me again.

"What am I going to do without you, Archimedes? Who will create things for me that simultaneously protect me and risk my life?"

"Fortunately, you don't have to ask yourself that question," he informed me and reached into his pocket. He pulled out a purple velvet pouch and handed it to me. "You'll know when you need it."

I looked at the bag, then back at him. "What does it do?"

"You'll find out then." He gathered me in another tight hug, whispered a final farewell, and walked away.

"You ready?" I asked Ally when he was gone. "I think it's about time I made curfew."

CHAPTER THIRTY-EIGHT

"How long do you think it will be until they tear this place down?"

Ally looked around the motel room that was my first home after escaping from The Deep. She shuddered, still not seeing in it what I did.

"Probably not long. I know you love this place, but it's pretty horrible."

"You can't appreciate its unique characteristics and charm."

"Black mold and asbestos aren't charming," she retorted.

"I'm still going to miss it," I admitted.

"I tell you what. We'll take a little more time to get settled and figure out life again, then you and I will go on vacation. A real vacation this time. No trying to hunt down supervillains or fighting monsters. We'll do a road trip and stay in really nice hotels that have clean sheets and hot running water."

"You're on. We never did get to Florida together. There are a couple of rides with my name written all over them."

"Deal. Are you ready to go?"

"Yeah." I looked around. "Splinter? Where are you, buddy?" He poked his head out of the drawer where he used to sleep. "You ready to go?"

He ran up to me, and I picked him up, cuddled him close for a second, then perched him on my shoulder. He was getting used to the idea of sitting there while we walked around out in public. Of course, there were still strange stares and occasional gasps. I told him it was because he was too stunningly beautiful for some people to handle.

We took a final look around the dilapidated hotel room, a tangible reminder of how far I'd come and what I was ready to leave behind, and walked out. Allie's car waited on the road, and we climbed in. The sun was setting around us, and the new wave of Charleston nightlife was starting to filter out onto the streets. But that wasn't what I was looking forward to. It was over. It was time to go home.

The car tires screeched slightly before bouncing up over the curb and sliding onto the grass of the front yard. I shot forward, planted my hands on the dashboard to stop myself, then snapped back and smashed my head into the cushion behind me. The car came to a rest, and I slowly turned my head to glare at Ally.

"Seriously? Still can't hit that turn reliably?" I asked.

"Nine times out of ten, I arrive perfectly fine. You've witnessed that," she argued.

I nodded. "I have. That still leaves one time out of ten that you don't.

I glanced out the window at the house to my side and sighed. They hadn't heard the commotion outside because the door was still closed, but lights on in the windows told me they were home. After the final battle, Archie and Ally went and retrieved my family from their safe spot and brought them back. At my request, they hadn't mentioned me before the battle in case I didn't live through it.

They had already dealt with the fear and worry of me being missing and them not knowing what happened to me, then the pain and heartache of having to decide I must be dead. I didn't want them to go through that again. It was easier if they didn't know my involvement in anything that was happening until we knew everything would be all right.

When it was finally over and they were safe at home, I realized I still wasn't ready to go back immediately. It was all I'd dreamed of and hoped for since the night I left, but when the time finally came, I couldn't bring myself to do it. I needed more time to wrap my head around this new reality and prepare myself for it. Tonight was the night.

"Are you ready?"

I nodded and took off my seatbelt, then leaned across the car and hugged her close. I should have said something, but the words didn't come. It was like nothing would properly express what I was feeling and wanted to tell her. But she knew, and she always would. For ten years, she didn't give up on me, and I knew she never would.

After she dislodged her car from the yard and drove away, I stood at the end of the sidewalk and stared at the house. Nervousness rolled through me, making my palms tingle and my stomach feel squishy. I didn't know what to expect.

There was no precedent for this, nothing that could have prepared me for this moment. What would happen when I got to the end of the sidewalk and stepped back into the life I left behind? Was it possible to build a new life after your old one ended?

I knew my family missed me. Ally told me how much they thought about me and the effort they put into trying to find me. She made sure I understood the gap my disappearance left in their lives and how happy they would be to know I was still alive and all right. In my heart, I knew that was true.

They loved me and wouldn't want me to be gone from their lives forever. But as I walked up the sidewalk and climbed onto the porch, there were still painful questions and spikes of doubt in my mind.

Because they loved me didn't mean they would be ready to welcome me right back into their lives. By now, they were used to the thought that I was dead. Their dynamic had changed and adapted to me not being a part of the family anymore outside of memories. Maybe there wouldn't be a place for me. Perhaps they wouldn't be receptive to fitting me back in and would rather I stayed gone.

Maybe I had changed too much, and they wouldn't be willing to accept the version of me that appeared back in their lives.

I was more afraid of this moment than anything else I'd ever faced in my life. I turned around and almost left, but then I smelled something. I stepped closer to the house again and drew in a deep breath. My heart sang. My stomach rumbled.

Dad was making tacos.

I heard laughter. Then I glanced down and saw Splinter looking up at me from the pocket of my new leather jacket. He bounced and chittered excitedly, encouraging me to keep going. I smiled at him.

"All right, boy. Here we go," I whispered to him.

I stepped up to the door and knocked.

THE END

Holy smokes!

You made it.

And, so did Sara Slick. Of course she did.

There are a lot of things that are difficult in the author world. Sometimes its pretty hard to get things started. But that's seldom the case.

Generally speaking, in my experience, the hardest thing to do is to finish. Finishing a day's writing. Finishing a book. And, hardest of all, finishing a series. It's why Lee and I have so many damned open loops out there.

Just this week we had a business meeting where we discussed all of the stories that we have started and never completed. (I mean the ones that never saw the light of day.) There's a hell of a lot of them. Out of the blue, I remembered one that neither of us had talked about for years. (Believe it or not... a *Forgotten Gods* spin off that follows a woman named Emma in the Southwest that is also encountering the return of the gods!!).

And a lot of them are really, really good.

There are plenty of published open loops you can read right now. *Steel City Heroes, Rise of Magic, The Jack Carson Stories*. We just can't bear to close them down—there's more story to be told!

So, from the beginning, Lee and I decided to do something different. Something odd. Something outside of our comfort zone. "Sara Slick was going to be four books and that is all," we said. And here I am writing the notes to you, our dear readers, wrapping the whole thing up.

With that in view, it's only appropriate to thank the many people that made this series possible. From Michael Anderle and the LMBPN family who published the books, to our beta readers who pushed us to make the stories better and better each time we wanted to hit publish, to the editors, advertisers, and ST Branton—who might just get some time outside of Lee's basement.

Thanks to all of them.

But there's no way we would do any of this if it weren't for you! So as we put this series to bed, I want to reiterate that Sara slick was written *for* you. It's really all about you. And we have nothing else to say but, from the very bottoms of our hearts, thank you.

Of course, I hope you want to join us and ST Branton for another round of kick ass stories.

If you do can follow us on Facebook, sign up for our mailing list, or follow us on Amazon. It won't be long until the next series is out, we promise you that. Because we are really, really good at starting things.

Best regards,

Chris Raymond

PS: Want to hear more from us? Sign up for our newsletter and also receive a FREE copy of *The Devil's Due*, our fast and fun thriller: https://www.subscribepage.com/chris_and_lee

PPS: Honestly... Enough attention and arm-twisting by enough fans, I'd consider more Sara Slick. Just don't tell ST Branton.

Sign up for Chris and Lee's newsletter for updates, new releases, and promotions. When you join the community, you'll get a FREE copy of their fast, fun thriller, *The Devil's Due:*

https://www.subscribepage.com/chris_and_lee

Want more snarky heroines? Well, Chris and Lee also have an urban fantasy series about the mythic gods return to earth in their series with ST Branton, *Forgotten Gods.* The tagline is: *The gods are real, and they're assholes.* And it couldn't be closer to the truth. This series is fun, fast, exciting, and a little irreverent.

Vampires, werewolves, and all manner of monstrous creatures serve the unknown powers of old, but the story centers on the humans who make the heroic choice to fight them. Join Vic and her crew as they attempt to save earth from the gods who want it back. You won't forget, Forgotten Gods.

Oh, and... it is an 8 book omnibus almost always on sale for silly cheap!

While you're at it, we really thing you should try the new and improved *Steel City Heroes*:

A mad scientist fighting the laws of man and nature.

A demon-monster of mythical proportions.

A corporate conspiracy that goes back more than a century.

The Steel City is in desperate need of a hero.
Happy Reading!!

ALSO BY CM RAYMOND AND LE BARBANT

Steel City Heroes Saga

Catalyst
Buy Catalyst

Corrosion
Buy Corrosion

Crucible
Coming Soon

Casting
Coming Soon

Jack Carson Stories

The Devil's Due
Buy The Devil's Due

The Devil's Wager
Buy The Devil's Wager

The Rise of Magic
* With Michael Anderle *

Restriction (01)